Lt. Col. Joe Keating of the 681st Glider Artillery was coming south with stragglers from the 194th and 681st. The motley unit had spent most of their time clearing German pockets in their path.

But as the column moved further south, a column of 150 Germans — with tanks and self-propelled guns — broke out of a patch of woods and attacked Keating's troops. The lieutenant colonel sent his men to cover and then ordered his 105 mobile guns and Sherman tanks to disperse.

The GIs dove off the opposite side of the road and into ditches, while the mobile vehicles veered left and right. Keating peered through his field glasses and watched the Germans emerge from some trees. Wehrmacht soldiers were following the armor and the Germans apparently hoped to run over the Americans with their tanks and self-propelled guns. Keating waited patiently and ordered the 105mm and tank teams to aim their guns across the road. The colonel waited until the rumbling Mark IVs and artillery came almost opposite them on the road. Then he cried to his gunners.

"Fire!"

LAST BRIDGE TO VICTORY

BY LAWRENCE CORTESI

ZEBRA BOOKS
KENSINGTON PUBLISHING CORP.

ZEBRA BOOKS

are published by

Kensington Publishing Corp.
475 Park Avenue South
New York, N.Y. 10016

First printing: June, 1984

Printed in the United States of America

LAST BRIDGE TO VICTORY

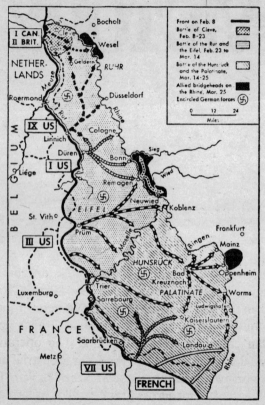

Front on Feb. 8	(solid line)
Battle of Cleve, Feb. 8-23	
Battle of the Rur and the Eifel, Feb. 23 to Mar. 14	
Battle of the Hunsrück and the Palatinate, Mar. 14-25	
Allied bridgeheads on the Rhine, Mar. 25	
Encircled German forces	(卐)

0   12   24
Miles

I CAN.
II BRIT.

Bocholt

Cleve

Wesel

NETHER-
LANDS

Geldern

RUHR

Roermond

Düsseldorf

BELGIUM

IX US

Linnich

Cologne

Düren

I US

Bonn

Sieg

Liége

Remagen

Wied

St. Vith

EIFEL

Neuwied

Koblenz

III US

Prüm

Frankfurt

Bingen

Mainz

Moselle

HUNSRÜCK

Bad Kreuznach

Oppenheim

Luxemburg

Trier

PALATINATE

Worms

Sarrebourg

Ludwigshafen

FRANCE

Kaiserslautern

Saarbrücken

Landau

Metz

VII US

FRENCH

Rhine

ALIGNMENT OF THE WESTERN ARMIES ON THE RHINE

CHAPTER ONE

On 18 March 1945, Gen. Dwight Eisenhower, commander in chief of all Allied forces in Europe, called a conference at his headquarters in Versailles, France. He summoned to his headquarters Field Marshal Bernard Montgomery and the commanders of the 21st Army Group from the northern sector on the Western Front.

In February, Montgomery had drawn up a plan called Operation Plunder. The operation was designed to overrun the Ruhr industrial area in northwest Germany and shorten the war. The Allies had swept across France and into Germany since D-Day in June of 1944. American and British troops had now reached the Rhine River in western Germany. However, except for the temporary breach at Remagen, the Allies had yet to establish a solid hold on the east bank of the river.

Among the Allied officers at the conference table besides Eisenhower and Montgomery were the 21st Army Group commanders: Gen. Miles Dempsey of the British 2nd Army, Gen. William Simpson of the U.S. 9th Army, Gen. Lewis Brereton of the Allied Airborne Army, and Gen. Hoyt Vandenburg, commander of the 9th Air Force.

"Gentlemen," Eisenhower began, "we've been stalled on the west bank of the Rhine all month because the bridge at Remagen is gone. The enemy has effectively destroyed all other bridges with their accurate artillery fire, and successful jet air strikes have stopped us from constructing any pontoon bridges to cross the Rhine. If we don't sweep through Germany soon, the enemy will start hitting us with their increasingly improved military hardware."

The Allied commanders knew the truth of Eisenhower's fears. The Germans had made ominous advances in weaponry during the past year. By March of 1945, the enemy had established strong jet aircraft units that were far superior to conventional planes. If the war lingered long enough, the Germans might amass enough jet fighter planes to wrest air superiority from the Allies. The Germans had also developed the snorkel innovation on her submarines and the U-boats were again taking a heavy toll against Allied shipping. Finally, the Germans had intensified their attacks with V-1 and V-2 rockets. If the enemy won time to produce enough of these V missiles and to improve the guidance systems of the weapon, they could cause havoc along the Western and Eastern Fronts.

General Vandenburg, commander of the 9th Air Force, enjoyed a five to one superiority over the Luftwaffe and his planes continually bombarded German airfields, railroad pikes, bridges, marshalling yards, and troop concentrations. But in recent weeks, well organized jet interceptor squadrons had often thwarted 9th Air Force bombing raids and the jet bomber units had caused serious disruptions against Allied units on the west bank of the Rhine.

The German ME 262 and ME 163 jet fighter planes had made a mockery of escorting U.S. P-51 Mustangs, the best Allied fighter plane of World War II. If the Germans delayed the Allies long enough, they could produce enough jets to regain control of the skies over Europe.

At his conference table, Eisenhower shuffled through some papers and he then continued. "Despite our best efforts and our vast superiority in men, planes, and hardware, the Germans continue to resist fiercely. We have grossly underestimated our enemy."

None of the generals at the table could disagree with the SHAEF supreme commander. In fact, the atmosphere was tense and pessimistic. Germany still controlled valuable sections of Europe and her population had shown no signs of casting off the Nazi government. Her industries still turned out substantial weapons from repaired or underground factories, especially advanced weapons. Further, 23 new divisions had been added to the German Armies of the West, including the Volkstrum People's Defense Forces who would most likely make last ditch stands in the cities and towns of West Germany.

"The Germans want time," Eisenhower gestured. "If they win another few more months to produce and throw enough of these new weapons at us, that might force us to give them favorable peace terms instead of insisting on unconditional surrender. That's why it's imperative that we cross the Rhine in force as soon as possible and push across Germany." He looked down at the papers in front of him before he spoke again.

"Field Marshal Montgomery's proposal is sound. Not only does the plan allow us to breach the river in strength, but a crossing in the Wesel area will enable us to sweep through the Ruhr. We can overrun the airfields in northwest Germany and we can occupy their industrial areas to put the enemy out of business."

The Ruhr industrial area in northwest Germany contained dozens of airfields, including jet airdromes. The Ruhr produced most of Germany's vital industry: 65% of her steel production, 56% of her coal resources, and 55% of her manufacturing in machinery, ball bearings, and other equipment to run her military machine. If the Allies occupied the Ruhr, they could decapitate Germany's production capacity and accelerate a Nazi collapse.

Eisenhower nodded to an aide who pulled

down a wall map behind him before the aide passed out small copies of the map to those at the table.

"As you can see," the SHAEF commander said, "Field Marshal Montgomery has worked out a major effort that includes an airborne assault as well as a river crossing assault. I'll ask the field marshal to fill you in on the details of this plan."

Montgomery, wearing his usual red beret, rose from his chair, nodded as the SHAEF commander, and then addressed the VIPs at the conference table. "Operation Plunder includes both a ground and air assault as General Eisenhower pointed out. We want to make certain we invest a deep bridgehead on the east bank of the Rhine."

The generals at the conference now listened at Montgomery reviewed his plan to occupy the Ruhr on the east side of the Rhine River. The 21st Army Group included both English and U.S. Forces, along with some Canadian brigades. Montgomery would use four British divisions, two Canadian brigades, and three American divisions in the initial crossings, with another dozen combat divisions as back up to follow the first waves. The British and Canadians would cross the Rhine with ground troops along a twelve mile front in the northern sector, and two American divisions would cross the Rhine along a ten mile front in the southern sectors. The British would drop their airborne division several miles behind the Rhine to the northward, while the Americans dropped their airborne division several miles behind the Rhine in the southern sector.

Among the American units, the 30th Infantry Division and the 79th Infantry Division would cross the Rhine south of Wesel to capture Dinslaken, Kirchhellen, and other fortified German positions before pushing east to the autobahn. The U.S. 17th Airborne Division's three regiments would drop north and east of Wesel to capture highway crossings, railroad pikes, the Issel River bridges, the Issel canal bridges and locks, and the Lippe River defenses. Then the U.S. airborne troops would push on to the autobahn.

Besides the several back up divisions to follow the vanguard units, the Allies would implant on the west bank of the Rhine some 3,400 British artillery pieces and 2,100 American artillery pieces to soften German defenses.

For the Americans, the U.S. Navy would provide more than 200 water craft to shuttle U.S. troops across the river. The boats would start fording the river at about 2200 hours, 23 March, and continue to shuttle troops, arms, and supplies across the Rhine until dawn. Hopefully, intense artillery barrages and heavy air strikes preparatory to the assaults would stem any major German resistance.

"These boats will carry from twelve to twenty-four men on one crossing, depending on the size of the boat," Montgomery told his audience. "They should not have much difficulty. We've determined that the entire stretch of front is quite level and clear, so we do not anticipate any problems with terrain. According to our navy people, we should have all troops and supplies ashore on the east bank by dawn unless we meet unusually heavy opposition, which we do not expect."

"The Rhine is only moving at a slow five knots at this time of year," General Eisenhower now spoke again, "so the current should not be a factor. Also, the shallowest depth is nine feet so the boats will have no problems."

"Now—the air drops," Montgomery spoke again, shuffling through some papers in front of him. "The 1st Allied Airborne Army will mount its troops in two areas. The British 6th Airborne Division will board their aircraft at East Anglia in England, and the American 17th Airborne Division will board their transports and gliders in the airfields south of Paris."

"Both of the air formations will rendezvous just south of Liege, Belgium," General Brereton suddenly spoke. The 1st Allied Airborne Army commander then gestured to the map. "Once these airborne units cross the Rhine, the 6th Division will make its jump right here on the plains north and east of Isselburg. A large force in this area will enable us to contain German forces who attempt to escape to the northeast into the Ruhr Valley."

Brereton pointed to the map again before he continued. "The paratroops and glider troops of the U.S. 17th Airborne Division will jump and land north and east of Wesel to seize key highway and railroad points between Hamminkeln and Wesel, while the glider troops will land east of

Wesel to seize the locks and bridges over the Issel Canal. The occupation of these areas will stop the Germans from getting reinforcements into Wesel."

"Are we certain the terrain is suitable for jumps and glider landings?" Gen. Will Simpson asked.

"We've reconnoitered the areas quite well," General Brereton answered the 9th Army commander, "and we don't expect the airborne troops to encounter too much difficulty."

"What about German interdiction?"

"These troopers won't be exposed for very long," Field Marshal Montgomery spoke again. "We expect to have our ground troops fully across the Rhine by morning and engaging the Germans before the paratroopers jump. The enemy will not have much time or many resources to also take on these airborne troops."

General Brereton then spoke again. "We've amassed the biggest fleet of gliders and transport aircraft ever assembled for a single operation. We'll be using approximately eight hundred transport planes and seven hundred fifty gliders to carry the 6th Airborne Division and their supplies to the drop zone. They'll also have the ammunition, guns, and vehicles they'll need when they land. They'll be taking off from East Anglia at about 0700 hours on 24 March to reach their drop zone at about 1000 hours."

Brereton paused, looked at a sheet in front of him, and then spoke again. "The 17th Airborne will be leaving their base south of Paris at about

0900 hours, rendezvous with the 6th Airborne aircraft, and then continue on. The 17th will also reach their drop zone at about 1000 hours. They'll have about nine hundred transport planes and six hundred gliders to carry their troops, equipment, cannon, vehicles, and supplies. The 17th, in fact, will try a unique innovation — the portable artillery. They'll carry with them the new fourteen pound 37mm gun for foot soldiers and the new one hundred fourteen pound 55mm guns for the same troops. The tanks will be the light Shermans with 75mm guns, along with tank destroyer vehicles, also with 75mm guns."

"You mean you're also dropping tanks?" General Simpson asked.

"Yes," Brereton answered. "The light tanks and TDs of the 681st Artillery Regiment will come in the gliders. The 681st will also have a substantial number of 105mm and 90mm guns that the artillery troops will reassemble once these weapons are on the ground. Of course, we'll need time to do these things." He looked at General Vandenburg, the 9th Air Force commander. "We'll need heavy air support almost continuously to protect the troopers because we don't know how heavily the Germans are entrenched in the Wesel area."

"We'll have plenty of planes," Vandenburg assured Brereton.

The 1st Allied Airborne Army commander remembered too well the heavy losses in Operation Market Garden last September. He did not want to squander his British and American paratroopers this time. Although not admitting so openly, General Brereton viewed Operation Plunder as a near carbon copy of the Market Garden affair that had failed so miserably. If he did not get plenty of air support, and if the ground troops did not seize key positions across the Rhine, the paratroopers could be in for real trouble.

"Hoyt," General Eisenhower now spoke again, "what kind of air support have you prepared for this operation?"

"We'll have at least two thousand fighters and bombers available from the 9th Air Force and the British 2nd Tactical Air Force."

"What about the Luftwaffe?" Montgomery asked.

"Our aircraft are constantly over West Germany as well as over other areas east of the Rhine," Vandenburg said. "We rarely see conventional 109 or 190 German fighter planes anymore, but we do occasionally run into those German jets. They've caused serious trouble against our bomber formations, but we've managed to avoid them most of the time. Fortunately, the enemy has very few of these jets in operation to intercept us very frequently. Anyway, we've been seeking out these jet bases. As soon as we find them, we'll knock them out."

"Are you certain these jet aircraft won't be a serious problem?" Montgomery asked.

"We hope not, sir," Vandenburg answered the 21st Army Group commander. "Our staff has worked out a good strategy to support Operation Plunder."

Montgomery did not answer, but he looked somewhat coldly at the 9th Air Force commander. Although the British field marshal was in charge of this operation, the American Hoyt Vandenburg was charged with all air operations. The idea had piqued Montgomery who had drawn the wrath of his own Air Marshal Arthur Coningham, whose 2nd Tactical Air Force came under the command of Vandenburg. The American air commander had simply given Coningham instructions for air support and the British air commander had been miffed by this arbitrary action from Vandenburg.

However, both Vandenburg of the 9th Air Force and Brereton of the 1st Allied Airborne Army, the two Americans, had insisted that Vandenburg direct the air phase of Operation Plunder in any way he saw fit. Brereton, especially, feared that poor or uncertain coordination between the USAAF and the RAF might endanger the operation. Montgomery had agreed to this concession in order to get the okay for Plunder.

"We intend to follow your airborne troops with one hundred fifty Liberators that will drop an additional five hundred forty tons of supplies daily to the paratroopers," Vandenburg continued, ignoring Montgomery's cool glance. "This much tonnage should be enough to keep the 6th and 17th Divisions supplied during the operation."

"What if they need more?" Montgomery asked. "Can you assure us they'll be supplied?" The field marshal was apparently hoping to embarrass Vandenburg.

"Sir," the 9th Air Force commander said, "we'll drop them one thousand tons of supplies a day; two thousand, if that's what you want."

Montgomery merely nodded, but Eisenhower grinned. "Very good."

"I'm still worried about those jet aircraft," Montgomery continued his barbs. "You said yourself, General, that our conventional fighters can't cope with them. How do you intend to deal with these jets? We can be sure the enemy will use such aircraft against this operation."

"I will suggest, sir," Vandenburg said, "that Air Marshal Coningham seek out and destroy these jet airbases with his RAF air units. These German air bases are known to be in northwest Germany in the 2nd RAF's zone of operation."

Montgomery did not answer.

"Do we have a clear picture of the German ground units in the Wesel area?" General Eisenhower asked.

"I can only tell you, sir," Vandenburg answered, "that our recon pilots have seen about a dozen scattered encampments in the area, along with small numbers of tanks and artillery. It's our opinion that the Germans don't have any more than two divisions to resist this operation."

Eisenhower nodded and then spoke again. "We'll begin our heavy artillery barrage at dusk on 23 March to soften up the east bank. Then I'd like aircraft to start hitting the drop zone areas with air strikes as long as possible, and with as many air groups as possible, to clear the terrain for the paratroopers and glider troops."

"I've assigned the 6th and 4th Air Divisions for such strikes," Vandenburg said, "four light bomber and four fighter-bomber groups. We'll also have a dozen fighter groups for cover and for interception, and we'll have several fighter-bomber groups on CAP continually during daylight hours to aid any unit that may need ground support."

"Fine," Eisenhower said. He then looked at Brereton. "Are all airborne units ready to go?"

"The 6th Airborne troops as well as the 17th Airborne troops have been well briefed and they've prepared themselves quite well."

The British 6th Airborne Division was a veteran unit. They had made several jumps behind enemy lines, including jumps in Sicily, France, and Holland. However, the division had usually been quite bloodied in these earlier operations, mostly because ground troops had failed to link up. But hopefully, such failures would not be repeated in Operation Plunder. The Allies believed they had such overwhelming superiority that the Germans could not stop the ground troops from linking up with the airborne troops. Further, the 6th and 17th Divisions would make their jumps and glider landings close to the river where Allied artillery on the west bank could furnish devastating cannon support.

The 17th Division had never jumped in combat, but the U.S. airborne troops were seasoned fighters. They had fought hard as ground troops during the Battle of the Bulge and during the

Ruhr Valley campaign. The men of the 17th were not likely to panic if they met intensive small arms fire or even artillery fire as they came down in their parachutes or in their gliders.

"Then we're ready to go?" Eisenhower asked.

Field Marshal Sir Bernard Montgomery nodded. "The artillery fire will open at dusk as you indicated, General," he gestured toward the SHAEF commander. "The boats will begin carrying men and supplies across the river at 2200. With any luck, we should have a firm foothold on the east bank by morning. At daylight," he looked at Vandenburg, "your light bombers and fighter-bombers should start softening the airborne drop zones."

"We'll have aircraft from the 9th Air Force and 2nd Air Force out by dawn," Vandenburg answered. "I'll have other RAF units out all day to find and destroy those jet airfields."

Montgomery nodded. "If all goes according to plan, the ground and airborne forces should link up by noon or shortly thereafter on the 24th."

"Okay," Eisenhower sighed, "let's get this show under way. Once we've established ourselves in the Wesel area, we'll be in good shape. If we draw enough enemy troops from other areas along the Rhine, that should make things easier for the other Allied army groups to the south of the 21st Army Group to make effective Rhine crossings of their own."

But the Germans had no intention of giving up Wesel or any other areas on the east bank of the Rhine. The Allied troops would meet stiff resistance, especially in the case of the Americans. For example, the 120th Infantry Regiment would find the 60th Grenadier Regiment troops of the 116th Panzer Division unusually tough. The U.S. 513th Parachute Regiment would meet stubborn resistance from the stalwart FJR 6 Regiment of the German 2nd Parachute Division, and the American 194th Glider Regiment GIs would meet a surprisingly determined force in the enemy Wesel Volkstrum Division.

CHAPTER TWO

In an elaborate country chalet, ten miles east of the Rhine, Gen. Johannes Blaskowitz maintained his Staff Hamburg, the headquarters of the German Army Group H. Included in this army group were the 1st Parachute Army, the 25th Army, and the Luftwaffe's Luftflotte II. The army group included three parachute divisions, two infantry divisions, two armored divisions, and Luftflotte II with a mere 500 aircraft, including 200 fighters. However, two gruppens with jet planes, JV 7 with ME 262 fighter bombers and KG 51 with AR 234 light bombers, were also in Luftflotte II.

On 19 March, the day after Eisenhower's conference at Versailles, Field Marshal Blaskowitz held a conference of his own with his two army commanders and Luftwaffe commander. The towns and woods north, east, and west of the field marshal's elegant chalet were dotted with tents and billets that housed some 85,000 troops under Blaskowitz's command. Present at the Staff Hamburg headquarters on this 19 March morning were Gen. Alfred Schlemm of the 1st Parachute Army, Gen. Gunther Blementritt of the 25th Army, and Gen. Erich Wilke of Luftflotte II.

"We have thus far stopped our enemies from crossing our sector of the Rhine River here in the northwest," Blaskowitz told his audience, "but the Allies have not given up." Blaskowitz pursed his lips and then continued. "A crisis appears evident here in the north. Our intelligence indicates that the enemy's 2nd Army Group is massing in force on the west bank of the Rhine opposite the Wesel area. Should enemy forces overrun our sector, they could sweep through the industrial Ruhr." He looked at Gen. Erich Wilke. "Has the Luftwaffe verified these disturbing reports?"

"I fear that aerial reconnaissance has confirmed your suspicions, Herr Field Marshal," Wilke said. "The British are mustering several divisions northwest of Wesel and the Americans are massing several divisions along a ten mile front west of the city. Luftwaffe pilots have also observed long trains of artillery moving toward the west bank."

"Where do you believe they may cross?" General Schlemm asked Blaskowitz.

The Army Group H commander turned to a

map on the wall behind him. "Unfortunately, almost the entire river bank north and south of Wesel between Dinslaken and Isselburg is favorable to land boats with troops and supplies. We can assume the enemy will attempt to seize railroad and highway areas about Wesel as quickly as possible. They will probably try to take Hamminkeln and Diersfordt as well as the key rail and road junctions in these areas."

"What of the Issel Canal?" General Blementritt asked.

"Yes," Blaskowitz answered. "I'm sure they want the canal as well as the bridges and locks over both the canal and Issel River. I am sure they will also attempt to seize the Lippe River bridges and defenses."

Blaskowitz scanned his commanders before he spoke again, "We must alert our troops throughout the entire Army Group H sector, including Wesel and Isselburg."

"Do we have enough combat units to stop a massive enemy assault?" General Schlemm asked.

"We will keep reserve units to the east, and such troops can reinforce any of our positions that need them."

The term reserve brought a tinge of doubt to the assembled generals. The 25th Army's two infantry and two Panzer divisions were badly under strength, with less than 40,000 men in this army. Further, they had barely enough rifles and machine guns to defend themselves, while the two Panzer divisions had less than 400 tanks between them. Army Group H had lost hundreds of men wounded, killed, or captured during the retreating battles eastward into Germany, and the Wehrmacht high command had failed to send replacements. Most of the Panzer troops would need to fight as infantry—if they could find enough weapons.

Only the 1st Parachute Army was close to strength, with nearly 30,000 men among the three divisions. Although the parachute troops had fought continuously along the Western Front since the autumn of 1944, they had been among the few units that withdrew to the east bank of the Rhine with minimal losses in men and equipment. Most of this success could be traced to General Schlemm's leadership and the adept ability of the paratroopers themselves. The paratroops were still well armed, with plenty of ammunition, artillery, and vehicles for mobility. They would play a key role in defending the east bank in the Army Group H sector.

But the paratroopers alone could not stop a massive Allied thrust. Blaskowitz would also need to use substandard, inexperienced troops such as the Volkstrum troops, home guards of older men and teen agers who had been too young or too old for regular combat units. The field marshal had in his Army Group H the Wesel Volkstrum Division that numbered about 10,000 men. The division, under Col. Frederick Ross, would defend the city of Wesel itself.

Finally, Luftflotte II had about 10,000 airmen among its various gruppens.

All total then, General Blaskowitz could count on 85,000 troops to defend his sector of the Rhine. This number was really quite ludicrous compared to the more than a million men that General Montgomery had amassed for Operation Plunder, although only about 150,000 of the Allied soldiers were actual combat troops. Further, the Germans would be entrenched in established defense positions, so that even with the superiority in men, hardware, and planes, the Allies would not have an easy time in this offensive.

The worst problem for the Germans was the overwhelming Allied air superiority. But even here, Army Group H had two consolations. First, the German troops long accustomed to heavy Allied strikes had learned to keep armor, supplies, and themselves well hidden from aerial assailants. Second, the two jet units of Luftflotte II could make tactical assaults with near impunity in critical areas where German ground troops were in danger of collapse.

General Blaskowitz now proposed his defense measures to the assembled army leaders at his Staff Hamburg headquarters. He used a pointer as he turned to the map on the wall behind him.

"You can see where our units should be encamped. We will have two regiments of the 15th Panzer Division here at Isselburg." He looked at General Blementritt. "They will defend the highways between Isselburg and Bocholt."

"Yes, Herr Kommandant," Blementritt answered.

"The 116th Panzer should be bivouacked here,

27

east of Hunxe," Blaskowitz continued. "They can rush troops eastward if the Allies attempt to seize the Lippe River defenses between Wesel and Hunxe." He then tapped another part of the map. "Here, between Wesel and Hamminkeln to the north, we will station the 2nd Parachute Division. They can defend the highway and rail links between Hamminkeln and Wesel. And, of course, the Wesel Volkstrum Division will defend the city." The field marshal now looked directly at Blementritt. "You have a regiment of your 116th Panzer Division encamped here, west of Hunxe and seven miles east of Wesel."

"That is Colonel Harzer's 60th Grenadier Regiment," Blementritt said.

"Would you agree, General, that enemy units will surely attempt to take the Lippe River defenses and cut off the waterway so that none of our reinforcements can reach Wesel?"

"Yes," Blementritt nodded.

"I would like you to use this regiment to protect the river defenses."

"The 60th Grenadier Regiment can do the job," the 25 Army commander said. "The troops of this regiment are known for their tenacity and determination."

Blaskowitz nodded and then looked at the commander of the 1st Parachute Army. "It is important that your parachute troops hold Hamminkeln and Diersfordt at all costs," the field marshal told General Schlemm. "Should we lose these roads and highway centers in the north, Wesel will be open to enemy troop movements while the areas will be closed to us, without the ability to send reinforcements to Wesel."

"I understand," the 1st Parachute Army commander said. "The FJR 6 Regiment is entrenched in defenses between Hamminkeln and Wesel, and other 2nd Parachute Division troops about Hamminkeln itself. I can assure you, Herr Field Marshal, these units will do whatever is necessary to hold the vital road and rail links."

"Excellent," the Army Group H commander said. "We will depend heavily on your parachute troops. Should we lose these vital communications, the enemy will be free to drive into the Ruhr Valley. We cannot allow this to happen."

"I will keep these paratroopers mobile," General Schlemm promised.

If Blaskowitz could count on anyone, he could count on the 1st Parachute Army troops. During the U.S. 9th Army drive to the Rhine, the 1st Parachute troops had done more to hurt, harass, and stall the Americans than any other German unit on the Western Front. As 9th Army troops pushed toward Elsdorf, a road junction on the route to the Rhine, Schlemm's troops had delayed more than four times their number in enemy forces, while other elements of Army Group H had successfully withdrawn across the Rhine.

On 2 March, when the American 5th, 84th, and 2nd Armored Divisions pressed toward the Krefeld Bridge, the last obstacle on the road to the Rhine River's west bank, Schlemm's troops had again put up a determined defense. A mere three to four understrength 1st Parachute Army battalions had held up the three U.S. divisions for three days, while the German troopers knocked out a dozen American tanks and a host of artillery pieces. The American drive had ground to a halt under heavy mortar fire, anti-tank guns, and sheer stubbornness on the part of the parachute soldiers.

When the 2nd Parachute Division under the capable Gen. Walter Gericke saw that they could not hold off any longer the overwhelmingly superior forces of the enemy, the paratroopers had blown the Krefeld Bridge to delay the Americans for another three days.

Then, on 7 March, a single regiment of the 2nd Parachute Division had held off two combat divisions of the Canadian 1st Army, including an armor division, for two days. Word had come from Hitler himself that the FJR 6 Regiment was to hold to the end. The regiment's commander, Oberst (Colonel) Friheer von der Heydte, had agreed as did his men. The regiment had held for two days until Kesselring himself finally persuaded Hitler to allow the withdrawal of these courageous, experienced combat troops.

Heydte and his men had then withdrawn across the Rhine, blowing the Wesel bridges behind them and denying the Canadians an opportunity to cross the Rhine River.

After addressing General Schlemm, Blaskowitz tapped another part of the map that was ten miles east of Hamminkeln. "The 15th Panzer Division has units here, to the northeast at Elms. I will use these troops to reinforce any other units wherever we feel that such reinforcements become necessary." He looked at Blementritt. "How many tanks does the 15th Panzer have?"

"Not many; about one hundred Tigers and Panthers," Blementritt said. "But while they are few, they are much superior to Allied armor. The Panzer units at Elm also have twenty-five or thirty field pieces, including 88mm and 120mm guns. I can assure you that this armor and cannon will be put to good use."

"Good," Blaskowitz nodded. "We may call on these troops to aid the parachute troops along the Hamminkeln-Wesel corridor."

The Army Group H commander now considered the city of Wesel itself. The Wesel Volkstrum Division, two brigades of home guards, were entrenched within the city, especially along the Rhine riverbank. After Blaskowitz tapped the map, he looked at General Blementritt. "Is it possible that your Volkstrum brigades can hold the city of Wesel?"

"We can only do our best," the 25th Army commander answered. "The young men and the older ones are willing to fight. They have seen our enemies destroy their homes, cause suffering among their families, and reduce their living conditions to a bare subsistence. They will fight any invaders and fight them hard."

Blaskowitz nodded and then looked again at General Schlemm. "Is it possible, Herr Schlemm, that you could assign a cadre to each of the Volkstrum companies that must defend Wesel? I have no doubt that these home guard soldiers will conduct themselves with valor. Still, they are inexperienced and they have been hastily trained for the most part. Perhaps it would be wise if troops from the experienced 1st Parachute Army joined these Volkstrum units to aid them in tactics for a defense of the city."

"Of course," Schlemm said.

Blaskowitz turned to Blementritt. "Do you agree with such measures?"

"Yes, Herr Field Marshal. In fact, I would welcome these cadres for the Wesel Division. Not only can they help us in tactics, but they would also be helpful in morale."

"Good," Blaskowitz said.

"I believe we can afford a battalion of troops from the FJR 26 Parachute Regiment for this effort," General Schlemm said. "I can assign a platoon of troops to each Volkstrum battalion. Not only will these soldiers reinforce the Wesel Division, but they can direct the Volkstrum troops in battle."

"Please make arrangements at once," Blaskowitz gestured, "so the cadres can join the Volkstrum companies as soon as possible."

General Schlemm nodded.

Blaskowitz now looked at General Wilke of Luftflotte II. "What may we expect from the Luftwaffe in the event the enemy attacks our sector?"

Wilke squeezed his face. "I must tell you, Herr Kommandant, that we have but five hundred aircraft available in our Luftflotte. We also have a shortage of fuel and pilots. I have continually pleaded with Reichmarshal Goering to send us more fuel, planes, and airmen, but thus far I have received only promises. I have also urged Field Marshal Milch to send us pilot replacements, but he too only makes promises. I do not know how much help we can offer in the face of heavy Allied air superiority."

"We must have air support if we are to successfully repel the enemy from the east bank of the Rhine," Blaskowitz said. "It is now almost certain that the enemy intends to make his next attempt to cross the Rhine in our sector. And why not? The Allies would like nothing better than to overrun the Wesel area and sweep through the industrial Ruhr, perhaps all the way to Hamburg. If we are to stop such an Allied assault, we must have help from the Luftwaffe."

"I can only say that we will do whatever we can," Wilke answered. "We cannot possibly mount enough aircraft to assault the enemy troop concentrations, their motorized columns, or their communications system, especially against their hordes of fighter aircraft. The best strategy, in my opinion, is to offer air support wherever one of positions is in danger of collapsing."

"I see," Blaskowitz said.

"In these crucial areas, where danger is imminent," Wilke said, "we will use a jet aircraft unit. Both our JV 7 gruppen and KG 51 gruppen will answer a call for air support within an hour."

"Can we depend on such support?"

"I have already notified Colonel Steinhoff of JV 7 to have his pilots on continuous alert. He has about fifty ME 262 jet aircraft. I have also been assured by Major Kowalaski of KG 51 that his Aredo bombers will be ready to fly on a moment's notice. Of course, we do have other air gruppens of conventional 109 fighter planes and 110 light bombers. These units will also be used wherever possible."

"Herr Wilke, have you assigned a liaison officer from each gruppen with each regimental headquarters?"

"It has been done," Wilke said.

"Very good," Blaskowitz answered. Then he straightened his tall, muscular frame and scanned the officers about the table. "Gentlemen, I cannot urge you strongly enough to do your duty. We of Army Group H may be the last hope for the fatherland. If we do not stop our enemies here, they will simply destroy us — our soldiers, our cities, our people, our nation. We have been assured by Herr Albert Speer, our minister of production, that advanced weaponry is now coming out of our underground factories at an accelerated pace, weapons that will overwhelm our enemies, despite their superiority in men and arms. We must delay the enemy as long as possible to give Herr Speer the time he needs to produce huge numbers of these new weapons."

The officers only listened.

"We in the Wesel sector are in a most unique position," General Blaskowitz continued. "Fortune has left to Army Group H the task of winning a victory the Fatherland needs so badly. True, the enemy will have countless troops and tanks and guns and aircraft. That means that each soldier must contain ten times his number in enemy soldiers," Blaskowitz gestured emphatically. "Each tank must destroy a dozen Allied tanks, while each artillery piece must silence ten enemy guns. And finally, each Luftwaffe pilot must be prepared to stop ten Allied pilots. I ask of you and your soldiers a tremendous task, but the Fatherland and our people will depend on us."

"We will succeed, Herr Field Marshal," General Schlemm said.

"My troops of the 25th Army will not falter," General Blementritt said.

"Every man in Luftflotte II will spare no effort," General Wilke promised.

Gen. Johannes Blaskowitz sighed. "All of you know your assignments." He shuttled his glance between General Schlemm and General Blementritt. "I expect you to meet with your division and regimental commanders to make certain they recognize their duties to defend our sector of the Rhine." He then looked at Wilke. "Your airmen must make a harsh effort."

"Yes, Herr Field Marshal."

Blaskowitz sighed again. "If there is no further business, then this conference is over."

Thus, Blaskowitz readied his commanders to defend their strip of the Rhine River. Only time would tell if Col. Walter Harzer of the 60th Grenadier Regiment, Col. Friheer von der Heydte of the FJR 6 Parachute Regiment, Col. Frederick Ross of the Wesel Volkstrum Division, and a host of other Army Group H unit commanders could successfully direct their troops against the expected Allied assault across the Rhine.

CHAPTER THREE

The U.S. 30th Infantry Division troops left their encampments on the Maas River at dawn, 23 March 1945. Their vehicles and equipment were heavily camouflaged to hide their eastward movement. Radio silence had begun as soon as the division's personnel boarded their 6x6 trucks and personnel carriers for the ride to the Rhine. The endless parade also included artillery pieces, weapons carriers, armored vehicles, and flat bed trucks carrying heavy bridge construction equipment.

The 21st Army Group staff had also created a dummy buildup in the area east of Dusseldorf and the Erft River in the hope the Germans would believe that the Allies were attempting to cross the Rhine in the Dusseldorf-Uerdingen

Zone. Further, Montgomery had delayed heavy bombardments of the Wesel target until the last moment.

The sun had risen high in the sky by midafternoon of 23 March. The motorized columns had been moving for several hours. In the rear of a U.S. 30th Division 6x6, Cpl. Les Belden, a demolitions man, and Pvt. Rex Anderson, a rifleman, both of G company sat quietly. Around them sat ten other men of Sgt. John Ramer's squad. The two GIs from 2nd Battalion, 120th Regiment, squinted into the bright sun overhead, relishing the warmth after the long, harsh winter in northwest Europe.

The two infantrymen had fought the Germans in the deep snow of the Ardennes, the bitter cold of the Huertgen Forest, and in the soggy mud of the Ruhr River valley. Now, they were again moving into combat. They looked at the long line of trucks behind them, as far as the eye could see; and in front of them—a similar endless train of vehicles.

Interspersed among the 6x6s and personnel carriers were artillery caissons, supply trucks, jeeps, amtracs, weapons carriers, and the long trailers carrying the boats that would float the GIs across the Rhine River.

Corporal Belden jounced on the hard seat and his satchel bag bounced against his hip whenever the 6x6 hit another rut in the countless potholes on this much traveled highway. The G Company dogface was tired and weary after the months of combat that had finally terminated after the capture of Steinstrass against stubborn German resistance. Anderson's company had knocked out eight enemy tanks and captured 200 prisoners. But instead of going on rest leave, the men of the 30th Division had spent two weeks at the Echt training area on the Maas River to prepare for the assault across the Rhine.

Belden cursed the U.S. Army. How come his unit kept fighting in this hostile weather through desolated forests, muddy plains, and utterly destroyed and deserted villages? Other GIs who had fought much less or not at all had enjoyed furloughs in Paris and Liege and Nancy.

Pvt. Earl Otto, a BAR man, also sat quietly in the rear of the 6x6. He simply fingered the trigger of his heavy weapon. Next to Otto, Private Anderson again squinted up at the sky. Then the G Company private looked at his squad leader. The tall, slenderly built John Ramer sat with a somber look on his face and stared into the empty landscape around him. Perhaps the sergeant also wondered why G Company, after so much continuous fighting, had not been sent to a rest area to the rear.

Private Otto studied the men with him and then looked at the squad leader. "Sarge, where do you think we're going?"

"Across the Rhine," Ramer answered brusquely. "Everybody knows that."

"Yeh, but where?" Anderson now spoke.

The non-com shrugged. "How the hell do I know where?"

The long convoy of U.S. vehicles ground to a

halt in the middle of another shattered German town. Anderson studied the surrounding rubble, so complete that he could not identify the destroyed structures as shops, stores, or homes. The private did not see a single person on the streets. He jerked when Capt. Charles Moncrieff, the company commander, barked sharply.

"Okay, all out! All out!"

The GIs scrambled from the truck as did other infantrymen from G Company, before the squads lined up in front of their vehicles. Then Moncrieff cried again. "You're in the German town of Wallach, two miles west of the Rhine River. We'll camp here for the rest of the day. At dusk, we'll march to the river bank and board LCIs for the Rhine crossing." The officer looked at Ramer. "Sergeant, make sure your men have ample ammunition, complete medical kits, and at least four K ration meals in their packs. Once across the Rhine, nobody knows how soon we can set up any kind of encampment."

"Yes, sir," Sergeant Ramer said. After the captain moved off, Ramer turned to Cpl. Les Belden. "Draw enough grenades, cartridges, any rations from supply to make sure every man has enough. God only knows when we'll get a good meal again, and I don't think we'll find any restaurants on the other side of the Rhine."

"Okay, Johnny," Belden answered the squad sergeant.

The men of G Company did not unpack their gear, but they only rested amidst the debris of Wallach. They would stay here until late evening when they would march to the Rhine, board boats, and ride across the river. Two full U.S. divisions and their supplies would make the crossing in the southern sector.

Sgt. John Ramer double checked Belden to make certain his men had plenty of sulfa powder, iodine, and bandages in their medical kits; ample cartridges for their M-1 rifles, BARs, and portable .50 caliber machine guns. And the non-com made sure each GI carried enough K rations. G Company hoped to be well entrenched across the river by late tomorrow afternoon, but Ramer was not confident. The slender sergeant remembered too vividly the unexpected, stubborn German defenses at Steinstrass, the endless buried mines in the Huertgen, and the heavy fire from accurate 88mm artillery as the GIs slogged across the Ruhr plains. There was every possibility that the men might find the same enemy resistance east of the Rhine, and perhaps worse, for this river was the last natural barrier to the open Ruhr plains.

When the squad non-com finished checking the men, he sat against a wall of a ravaged building to drink some coffee prepared by company cooks. Cpl. Les Belden joined him.

"What does G-2 say about the krauts across the river, Johnny?" Belden asked the squad sergeant.

"The same old crap," Ramer answered. "They say our air units have knocked out the enemy positions. The flyboys always claim they bombed and strafed the shit out of 'em but when we get

41

there, the krauts fight like the air force never touched 'em."

"The pricks," Belden cursed. "They must be like roaches. You just can't kill 'em."

"Yeh," Ramer nodded. "We'll probably have to dig 'em out 'a trenches and out of the rubble and holes — one by one, or maybe a couple at a time."

"We may not clear our section by tomorrow night," Belden said.

"Maybe not," Ramer answered. "That's why the squad needs enough rations for at least a couple of days."

The two men looked up when they heard the sound of planes — American P-47s from the U.S. 9th Air Force. The Thunderbolts whined like squealing hawks as they zoomed over Wallach and then dropped out of sight. Less than a minute later, Belden and Ramer heard the distant rattle of machine gun fire and the echo of countless explosions. The P-47s were strafing and bombing on the east bank of the Rhine. When the sounds diminished, Belden looked at Ramer.

"Johnny, maybe those air jockeys really did get the krauts this time."

"Ah, they'll never get 'em," Ramer gestured in disgust. "No matter how many bombs they drop, or how much strafin' they do, we always find the bastards waitin' for us."

The two men spent the rest of the afternoon loafing or making occasional checks on the GIs of the squad. At dusk, the G Company cooks, over open gas stoves, prepared the troops a hot supper from canned bully beef and dehydrated potatoes. The fare was hardly appetizing but the men ate ravenously. All of them knew this meal would be their last hot meal for perhaps a couple of days. And for some of the GIs in G Company, this meal would certainly be their last.

Dusk of 23 March moved steadily into late evening. In the darkness, a soft breeze came up to wisp across the rubbled streets of Wallach, while an emerging three-quarter moon dimly lit the silhouettes of the town's smashed buildings that looked like grotesque ebon shapes. Some of the GIs tried to sleep, but most of them were too tense or too frightened for slumber. They mostly paced about the area or chain smoked cigarettes. A few drank wine from bottles they had miraculously found in cellars somewhere, bottles they had carried with them for many weeks over many miles.

Finally, at 2330 hours, Lt. Art Saalfield, the G Company executive officer, moved among the GIs. "Okay, saddle up! We're moving out!"

Moments later, Ramer's squad made a final gear check and then marched through the rubble of Wallach, across an open field, and then along a narrow road. Soon, the black outlines of wrecked structures loomed ahead—buildings that had been pulverized by shelling and bombing. The town was Mollen, another utterly destroyed village that had been totally deserted by its residents.

The squad weaved through the German town to the banks of the Rhine where they heard thumping canisters arch through the dark night like oversize Roman candles. A moment later, the cannisters exploded above the water and huge clouds of dense mist filled the area along a mile length of the river. The odor of chemical smoke then drifted westward and stung the nostrils of the GIs. Hopefully, the heavy screen would hide the movements of the troop laden LCIs that would soon putter across the river.

At 0030 hours, 24 March, Captain Moncrieff gestured to his men. "Okay, climb aboard; climb aboard."

Ramer's squad clambered into the same LCI for the ride across the river. Within two days, Sgt. John Ramer, Cpl. Les Belden, Pvt. Rex Anderson, and Pvt. Earl Otto would conduct themselves with unusual valor. Three of them would earn the DSC (Distinguished Service Cross), but two of them would be dead.

Far to the rear, at this same midnight hour, at the Achiet Airfield outside of Paris, Pvt. Paul Hines of New York City, Pvt. Ralph Walley of Little Rock, Arkansas, Pvt. Stuart Stryker of Portland, Oregon, and Pvt. Walt Leonard of East Palestine, Ohio, were still awake. They loitered in their relatively comfortable quarters, a pitched tent with four army cots. These paratroopers from E Company, 513th Regiment, U.S. 17th Airborne Division, could see the countless rows of C-47 transport planes that sat on the wide field like huge quiet black spiders. These dormant aircraft would burst into screaming whines sometime tomorrow when crew chiefs ignited the engines for pre-flight warm-ups.

The four GIs had been a part of the 17th Airborne for several months, but they had yet to jump into combat. The quartet had fought as infantrymen during the German Ardennes offenses, having joined reinforcements who had pushed back the enemy during the bitter Battle of the Bulge. The four privates had been green troops at the time, and they had faced battle-tested, long experienced SS Panzer Corps troops west of Bastogne. But the GIs had risen to the task and forced the enemy to retreat. These paratroopers had also fought in the Huertgen Forest in January and then returned to Achiet. Here, for the past month, they and others of the 513th Regiment had undergone specialized training for their first jump into combat, the upcoming assault across the Rhine River.

Private Hines stared at the black shapes of C-47s on the field and he then looked at Private Walley. "Ralph, how soon do you think we'll leave?"

"I don't know," Walley said.

"At dawn maybe?" Hines asked.

"A little later, I think," Pvt. Walt Leonard now spoke. "We're supposed to make the jump at midmorning, and they say the Rhine is about two hours away."

"I wish to hell I could sleep," Hines said. "I got a feeling we ain't gonna get any sleep for a long time once we climb into those transports."

"Do you think we'll meet a lot of opposition, Stu?" Walley asked Stryker.

"I'm not an expert," Stryker answered. "But

I'd guess those krauts might be awful stubborn in their own homeland on the other side of the Rhine. They won't give up without a fight."

"But they had the shit kicked out of 'em since the Bulge," Walley said.

"That don't make no difference," Walt Leonard said. "They always fight like hell."

"Don't worry about it," Stryker said. "Try to get some sleep."

"I can't sleep," Hines said again. He stared once more beyond the tent at the black shapes sitting quietly on the open airfield. He knew that in a few hours he'd be jumping from one of the planes right into the middle of enemy territory, and perhaps into withering gunfire. Hines had heard plenty about the near massacre of the 82nd Airborne in their jump into France on D-Day, and the heavy losses of the 101st Airborne on that jump into Arnhem last September during Operation Market Garden.

Hines felt an intuitive fear. Even he, a mere dogface, knew of Field Marshal Montgomery's record of failures in airborne operations. The British commander had insisted on the devastating jump on D-Day and he had wheedled permission for the near fatal Market Garden jumps in Holland. The young private was convinced that this Britisher was a loser — and now this loser had forced the 513th into a jump across the Rhine that could be even more lethal than the leaps into Normandy and Holland.

For several minutes, Pvt. Paul Hines stared from the tent. When he turned to look at his companions again, he saw Walt Leonard dozing off and Pvt. Ralph Walley already fast asleep. Strangely, Stu Stryker had risen from his cot and walked out of the opposite side of the tent to peer into the darkness. Hines ignored the fellow GI, flopping and stretching out on his cot. However, he now hoped he would not fall asleep because if they awoke him after a short one or two hour nap, he would be tired all day—something Hines knew he could not afford while jumping into enemy territory.

At 0700 hours, 24 March, Capt. Harry Kenyon, the E Company commander, and Lt. Dave McGuire, the company executive officer, sat in 2nd Battalion headquarters with other officers. Lt. Col. Allen Miller, the battalion commander, was issuing last minute instructions for the jump across the Rhine.

"You must be absolutely sure of your part in this operation," he pointed to a map behind him on the wall. "Jump point is here and our target is to reach these areas on the railroad pike and highway between Hamminkeln and Wesel. Our objective is to seize the areas to stop any Germans from using the highway or railroad to send reinforcements into Wesel."

"What about artillery support, Colonel?" Captain Kenyon asked.

"The 681st Field Artillery will send us one of their battalions from their landing area to the south. The battalion will include tank destroyers, light tanks, and mobile guns."

The E Company commander nodded.

Lieutenant Colonel Miller moved his finger about an area on the map in a circular motion. "There's supposed to be plenty of open terrain here to jump; not only for the 513th Regiment, but also for the 507th Regiment. They'll be dropping east of the woods around Diersfordt northwest of Wesel. Their job is to cut off communications over the highway between Wesel and Hamminkeln. We'll be jumping east of the woods to seize the railroad between the same two towns."

"What kind of opposition can we expect?" Lieutenant McGuire asked.

"Nobody knows for sure," Miller answered the E Company executive officer. "We hope our heavy artillery and continual air strikes will either destroy any German defenders or drive them off."

None of the officers answered their battalion commander, for they had experienced enough combat to understand a sobering truth: the Germans never faded away, no matter how many shells whooshed into their midst, nor how many bombs whistled into their positions. Captain Kenyon knew that cannon and air strikes often seemingly flattened enemy defense positions to rubble, but still, somehow, the gray clad Wehrmacht soldiers rose out of the pocked earth or powdered debris to fight tenaciously.

The E Company commander licked his lips. He expected nothing less from the Germans this time, and, in fact, he suspected the enemy would be more stubborn here than anywhere — for the Rhine was the last protective barrier into the heart of the German homeland.

At the same 0700 hours, the sudden ignition of aircraft engines exploded in deafening din at the huge Achiet airbase. 513th Regiment troopers who had not yet awoke jerked from sound sleep and sat upright on their cots. Moments later, the rasping voice of T/Sgt. John Queenan echoed through the E Company campsite.

"All out! All out for roll call in five minutes! Five minutes!"

Private Hines, Leonard, Stryker, and Walley were already dressed for none of them had slept soundly during the night. They soon joined other GIs from E Company on this cool morning to line up for roll call. In the Wesel campaign, two of these privates would win Silver Stars and one would win a Congressional Medal of Honor. But two of them would be dead.

On the evening of 23 March, south of Achiet at the sprawling troop carrier base of Sonsbeck, the men of the 194th Glider Infantry Regiment were in their tent sleeping quarters. Some of the men slept, but others didn't. These soldiers of the 17th Airborne Division felt as apprehensive over the upcoming Rhine battle as did other American GIs.

However, in a four man tent of C Company, 1st Battalion, S/Sgt. Clinton Hedrick lay asleep on his cot along with three other C Company non-coms: S/Sgt. Tom Martin, Sgt. Clem Noldau, and Sgt. William Woolfort. These men would lead platoons and squads of men in the operation across the Rhine as they had led men in the Ardennes, in the Huertgen, and across the Ruhr Valley.

The quartet slept rather soundly, despite their tenseness for the upcoming battle and their responsibilities for the GIs under them. But after so much war and so much heartache, they had grown callous and they now looked on dead GIs as no different than dead branches that had fallen from a tree. The non-coms had simply conditioned themselves to cry "medic" when a man got hit and writhed from painful wounds.

S/Sgt. Clint Hedrick had already won two medals, a Bronze Star with a cluster. He had earned the first during the fighting in the Huertgen when he and three other GIs captured a machine gun nest, and he had won the second Bronze Star when he led several men to safety during a German counterattack. By the time the 17th Airborne began its training for Operation Plunder, Hedrick had been promoted to staff sergeant to lead E Company's 3rd Platoon.

Tom Martin had been a non-com for nearly two years and a staff sergeant leader for little over a month. He had saved his squad from a wipeout during the Battle of the Bulge, and he had led them out of a trap in the Huertgen Forest fighting. He had then become C Company's 1st Platoon non-com.

Sgt. Clem Noldau had been a private when he first went into combat in the Battle of the Bulge. He had captured a half dozen Germans, taken over his unit when the squad leader got hit, and he had successfully repelled a German patrol. He had won a Silver Star and he now commanded a glider infantry squad.

Sgt. Bill Woolfort had also fought in the Bulge, the Huertgen Forest, and the Ruhr. He had shown exceptional leadership in combat to win promotion to sergeant and command of a squad.

At 0600 hours, 24 March, Lt. Al Richey, C Company's executive officer, ambled slowly past the rows of tents where men still slumbered soundly. Richey had only slept about five hours during the night and he now paced through the brightening campsite with a mixture of uneasiness and anticipation. He feared for the men of his company, but he wanted to get the job over with.

The first lieutenant stared at the dormant gliders on the huge field and he then looked up at the three-quarter moon that was now paling like a waning street lamp in the emerging daylight. The wisping breeze felt cold on this early spring morning and the lieutenant shivered. Richey moved about the area for about a half hour when the explosion of C-46 aircraft engines echoed across the flat landscape. The sudden high pitched whines was Richey's cue, and he headed straight for the non-com tent to awaken his sergeants. But Tom Martin was already awake and rousting the others from their cots. The sergeant turned when he saw the officer approach.

"They're getting up, sir," the platoon non-com said.

"Good," Richey nodded. "Have the men out

51

for roll call in five minutes. Then get them to chow and gear them up. We're supposed to board our gliders at 0800."

"Yes sir."

"Be sure the men have plenty of ammunition, six grenades, ample K rations, and full medical kits. God only knows when we'll settle again."

"We'll take care of it, sir."

The GIs of Martin's 1st Platoon as well as other troopers of the 194th Glider Infantry Regiment did not like these flimsy craft with their thin skinned, wooden frames. The gliders were too weak and if they hit a hard obstruction on landing, they often fell apart. The troopers had practiced extensively on these CG-4s but they never trusted them. The GIs had heard that the gliders could fall apart from even heavy machine gun fire, and a hit by a German 88mm anti-aircraft shell would disintegrate one of these Waco CG-4s.

Yet if the target area crawled with heavily armed Germans, these 194th Regiment troops stood a better chance of survival by coming into the ground inside a glider rather than by floating slowly to earth at the end of slowly descending parachutes.

By 0645 hours, the GIs of E Company had finished breakfast, a good hot meal and perhaps the last meal for some of them. Then the GIs washed and geared up before lining up in front of their tents at Sonsbeck. They listened to their company commander, Fred Wittig, as he issued final instructions.

"Make sure you have plenty of ammo, and make sure your medical kits are full. You should have at least four K ration cartons. We could have another meal tonight, but only if we overcome enemy resistance and secure our objective. We'll be dropping about ten miles east of the Rhine, just northeast of Wesel. The 194th will have two goals. First, we are to seize the locks on the Issel Canal to stop any reinforcements from coming into Wesel. Then we advance on Wesel itself from the north to help the Canadians and our own 30th Infantry to clear the city. Or, they may send us east after any retreating enemy troops."

The men of C Company only listened.

"Listen carefully to your officers and non-coms, and follow their orders faithfully," Captain Wittig continued. "They've got the experience and leadership, and you've got to depend on their judgment."

The C-47 engines whined smooth and clear now, for the engines were fully warmed up. One C-47 would tow a pair of gliders each and hopefully release them to a safe landing before German guns could blow them out of the sky.

At 0750 hours, Captain Wittig looked at his watch. "Okay, let's go. May God be with all of us."

Then, the C Company commander headed for a glider as did Lieutenant Richey, Staff Sergeant Martin, Staff Sergeant Hedrick, Sergeant Woolfort, and Sergeant Noldau. Among these six officers and non-coms of C Company, 194th

Glider Infantry, one would win a CMH (Congressional Medal of Honor), two would win DSCs, and two of them would die in battle. In fact, C Company would engage in one of the most vicious fire fights of the European war.

CHAPTER FOUR

The Rhine River has always been one of the most romantic lengths of landscape on the European continent. The valley had long fascinated visitors, and the German people had always been proud of the area. The legends surrounding the Rhine were best exemplified by the tale of Lorelei who had thrown herself into the river near St. Coar in despair over an unfaithful lover. She then became a siren who lured fishermen to their deaths as a means of revenge against all men.

In time, the legend developed into the so called Watch-Out-For-Lorelei warning for all those who sailed on the Rhine. The watch out myth then warped into a new meaning, a Watch-on-the-Rhine against all of Germany's traditional enemies from the west, especially France.

Hitler used the Watch-on-the-Rhine slogan as a rallying cry to whip up patriotism for the Nazi dictator's military adventures. Ironically, the first German defiance of the Versailles Treaty began at Wesel in 1937, where, before the cheers of supporting civilians, Hitler sent his troops across the river and into the Rhineland to scorn the World War I surrender terms. When the French and British failed to react, the German Fuhrer launched his series of annexations in Central Europe, including Austria, the Sudetenland, and finally Poland.

In March of 1945, it was now a battered German army that answered the Watch-on-the-Rhine rallying cry. Further, the Germans now faced overwhelming Allied military forces, and no civilians lined the streets of Wesel to cheer the Wehrmacht. Nonetheless, the Nazis still considered the Rhine its protective moat against her enemies from the west. Only after extensive pleas had Hitler allowed Field Marshal Blaskowitz to withdraw the final elements of his German Army Group H behind this moat and prepare defenses to meet the next enemy thrust.

Between Wesel and Hunxe, elements of the 116th Panzer Division were stretched out in defense pockets along the Lippe River. Unfortunately, the division had few tanks or other armored vehicles.

The 116th Greyhound Division had seen action on the Western Front for many months. Most recently, the Greyhounds had fought the Americans during the Ruhr River campaign.

They had then defended the area along the southern stretches of the Maas River during the Allies' Operation Grenade. And, despite the lack of men and tanks, the 116th Panzer had held out for several days before overwhelming odds had forced them to retreat. The Panzer troops had also held out at one of the last defenses west of the Rhine before they had finally retreated into Wesel, blowing bridges behind them.

Now, the Greyhounds had drawn the job of defending the area east of Wesel, including the crossings on the Lippe River and all roads that skirted this waterway.

Gen. Zengen Waldenburg, commander of the 116th, had spent most of the day, 23 March, in visiting the various defense positions. At dusk, he stopped to speak to Col. Walter Harzer, commander of the division's 60th Grenadier Regiment, and the regiment's 2nd Battalion commander, Maj. Sepp Krafft. The 60th Grenadiers had set up positions along the Lippe River from the railroad south of Wesel to the highway east of Hunxe. The regiment had about a dozen Mark IV medium tanks and most of the regiment would need to defend the area as infantry troops.

"Colonel," Waldenburg said to Harzer, "it is vital that the enemy does not seize any of the river points. In the event the Anglo-Saxons breach the Wesel defenses, or any defenses along the east bank of the Rhine, we will need to bring in help. Many of these reinforcements will come east over the Issel and Lippe Rivers. It is important, therefore, that these arteries remain secure."

"We will do our best," Colonel Harzer said. "Major Krafft and his 2nd Battalion troops are well entrenched in our sector. We have established defenses around the juncture of the railroad pike and the Lippe River, including many mortar teams, artillery units, and four Tiger tanks. These men are well experienced, Herr General, and they are determined to hold their positions to the end."

General Waldenburg looked at Major Krafft. "I hope your soldiers will hold to the end. I need not tell you, Major, what will happen if the Allies cross the Rhine and force us to abandon our positions. The industrial Ruhr of northwest Germany will be at the mercy of our enemies. If we lose the Ruhr, our cause will be lost."

"I understand, Herr General," the major said.

Waldenburg turned to Colonel Harzer. "I hope that other commanders in the other battalions of your 60th Grenadiers have the same determination as has Major Krafft."

"They do," Harzer answered, "I can assure you."

The 116th Panzer general shuttled his glance between Harzer and Krafft with a tinge of admiration. He remembered these Panzer officers well from the battle of Arnhem in Holland during the Allies' abortive Operation Market Garden. Harzer and Krafft had played key roles in directing Panzer tank forces and infantry soldiers during the Allied airborne assaults. The Greyhound Division's 60th Regiment had lacerated British paratroopers during that battle, slaughtering hundreds of English soldiers and capturing entire companies before driving the Tommies off in utter defeat. The general grinned at Harzer.

"We tasted sweet victory against the British at Arnhem last September when they found the Greyhounds too much for them. I believe we can repeat this victory in the Wesel area."

Harzer frowned. "Is there a possibility the Allies will make an airborne assault as well as an assault across the river?"

"We have no evidence of such an enemy intent. All of the reports indicate that the Allies will mount a large assault only across the river."

"Still," Major Krafft said, "we have vast stretches of open ground north and east of Wesel. This is ideal terrain for parachute jumps."

"I cannot believe the Allied commander Eisenhower will allow Montgomery to make further airborne drops," Waldenburg shook his head. "The Allies have never succeeded in parachute operations, not in Sicily, not in Normandy, and certainly not in Holland. In fact, we know that American parachute troops were fighting as infantry soldiers in both the Ardennes and Ruhr Valley."

"I hope you are correct, General," Harzer said, looking up at the sky. "Our troubles will be critical enough if the Allies force the Rhine in the Dinslaken-Wesel-Isselburg sector. I dread to think of the consequences if they cut us off in Wesel."

"Should they make a parachute drop, Colonel," Wallenburg said, "I believe our own parachute troops will engage such enemy airborne troops. In your own case, simply make certain that your own grenadiers protect successfully the Lippe River defenses."

"Yes, Herr General," Colonel Harzer said.

Gen. Zengen Wallenburg then continued on to check other regiments and battalions of his 116th Greyhound Panzer Division. He tried to bolster morale, charge his men with courage, and exhort them to fight to the last. The 116th commander, despite the retreat of German armies since the Battle of the Bulge, still believed he could stop the Allies east of the Rhine. He hoped to inflict such heavy casualties on the enemy that the Allied troops would be forced to retreat—as they did at Arnhem last September.

As the evening of 23 March wore on, Col. Walter Harzer and Maj. Sepp Krafft rechecked their soldiers on banks and bridges of the Lippe River to make certain they were prepared both mentally and physically to engage their enemy. Harzer was certain the Allies would launch an attack within the next day or two.

The 60th Grenadier commander had guessed right. In the wee hours of the morning, dozens of boats would hit the river banks south of Wesel before the American GIs drove swiftly eastward. The men of the 30th U.S. Infantry's 120th Regiment, soldiers like Captain Moncrieff, Sergeant Ramer, Colonel Belden, Private Anderson, and hundreds of other Americans would be plodding in column eastward to capture the vital Lippe River defenses. It remained to be seen if the troops of the 60th Grenadier Regiment would stop these infantrymen of the U.S. 120th Regiment.

North of Wesel, the troopers of the German 2nd Parachute Division had spread themselves out in dozens of defense positions around Hamminkeln and southward toward Wesel itself.

The 2nd was perhaps one of the most capable German combat units of World War II. The division's commander, Gen. Walter Gericke, had probably seen more action than any German officer of the 3rd Reich. Gericke had made his first drop in 1940 at the Vordinborg Bridge in Holland, and then at Dordrecht, also in Holland. By the Crete campaign in 1941, he had risen to the rank of lieutenant colonel and his battalion had made the jump at Maleme to rout the British defenders.

Gericke had later commanded a regiment of the 7th Parachute Division in Russia, where his unit had suffered heavy losses in the Ukraine. By July of 1943, he had joined the 2nd Parachute Division, whose regiments were fighting in both Italy and Russia. He won command of the 11th Parachute Division in January of 1945, but with heavy losses during the Huertgen and Ruhr fighting, the remnants of the division had joined the equally depleted 2nd Parachute Division and Walter Gericke had assumed command of this new unit with the rank of general.

2nd Parachute troops had been among the last

Germans to fight the Allies from positions west of the Rhine River. In this last battle, the 2nd had ripped apart the U.S. 2nd Armored Division in the town of Verdingen. Principally responsible for this win over the Americans was Col. Friherr von der Heydte who commanded the division's FJR 6 Regiment.

Heydte had first seen combat as an infantry soldier and in 1940 he had volunteered for parachute training, later leading a company in the airborne drop on Crete. His men had been the first troops to enter the British stronghold of Canae to capture this strategic port city. Heydte had then joined FJR 6 in Cologne in 1944 and his regiment had fought in Normandy with such tenacity that FJR 6 had earned the name "Lions of Carentan." But slowly and surely, the unit had retreated across France before superior Allied forces, with the regiment sustaining heavy losses along the way. The colonel himself had suffered a severe arm wound.

In the autumn of 1944, FJR 6 had taken up positions at the Allard Canal. And now, in March, Heydte and his FJR 6 troops had been assigned the task of protecting the vital road junction east of the Diersfordter Forest, so that reinforcements could move west over the Issel Highway or south to Wesel.

At 1900 hours, 23 March, Gen. Walter Gericke called a final conference with the 2nd parachute Division's three regimental commanders, including Friherr von der Heydte of FJR 6. "There is little doubt that the enemy intends to force a crossing of the Rhine in the Army Group H sector. The enemy attempted to deceive us into thinking he would force a Rhine crossing in the Dusseldorf-Verdingen zone, but our intelligence and aircraft reconnaissance reports are clear. There is a possibility the Allies may strike within the next twenty-four hours anywhere between Isselburg and Dinslaken, including Wesel itself. So we must be fully prepared. We have our regiments deployed around Hamminkeln and the Diersfordter Forest. Should fighting become intense inside Wesel, the highway and railroad from Isselburg and Hamminkeln will be vital to bring reinforcements into the city."

"Will our division furnish the reinforcements?" Colonel Heydte asked.

"No," the general answered. "The 15th Panzer Division at Elms will send units to any area that becomes critical. Also, the 84th Division has its troops at Gahlen and they too can send units to fill any gaps in our defenses. Finally, the 8th Parachute Division is above Isselburg and these units can attack in force on the enemy's northern flank. The duties of our regiments are clear: to protect Hamminkeln, Diersfordt, and the communications between Hamminkeln and Wesel."

"What of the Luftwaffe?"

General Gericke pursed his lips. "It is no secret that the Lufftwaffe can be of little help. The Allied air forces are simply too many in numbers. Still, we have been assured by Field Marshal Blaskowitz that two Luftwaffe jet gruppens will be at our disposal. These aircraft have already proven their superiority even against ten times their number in conventional aircraft. Further, our jet units have created severe psychological harm to Allied ground troops. The field marshal has established a liaison between the various division headquarters and the jet gruppen headquarters. A fleiger oberlt from KG 51 has been assigned to our 2nd Division to coordinate tactical air support as needed from the Aredo bombers." He paused and then continued. "Is there anything you need? Are there any questions?"

"Only one, Herr General," Colonel Heydte said. "Is it possible the Allies will attempt an airborne drop in conjunction with an assault across the river?"

"We have no reports of such enemy plans," Gericke said, "and let us hope they do not drop airborne troops behind us, perhaps on the Gahlen plains. But one never knows. You must prepare yourselves for anything. Make certain your units have ample supplies and ammunition, and make certain that artillery and mortar units have a sufficient supply of shells." He then looked at a map and ran a finger over the chart. "I cannot help but think that the enemy's first objective will be to seize the positions held by our division, and so block any reinforcements from going into Wesel. It is important that our troops thwart any attempts to capture these points."

"We will do what we must, Herr General," Colonel Heydte said.

"Good," the 2nd Parachute Division commander nodded. "Return to your units. Make a final check on your defenses and remind your troops of their duties."

At the same 1900 hours, 23 March 1945, Lt. Heinz Deutsch and Sgt. Heinrich Shafer stood on one of the signal bridges over the Diersfordt railroad tracks that ran southward into Wesel. The two men were the officer and non-com in charge of A Company, from FJR 6. They could clearly see the defenses in the town of Platte where the railroad and highway crossed, and they could faintly see the silhouettes of battered buildings in Wesel, some four miles beyond. The black shapes looked like craggy rocks rising out of the ground. The lieutenant and his ober-feldwebel had just completed a check on their machine gun teams posted at either end of the bridge. Now the duet from A Company had taken a short respite to stand in the middle of the bridge, a six feet wide and 30 foot long span that arched over the railroad pike.

Deutsch and Shafer were veteran paratroopers with extensive combat experience. The 24-year-old lieutenant had seen his first action in the bitter fight at St. Lo, France, in July of 1944, and he had fought in the retreating battles across France. He had also fought in Holland during Market Garden, where his unit had destroyed several Allied light tanks. Now, Deutsch had primed himself for still another fight. Ober-feldwebel Shafer had been in the Wehrmacht since 1936 and he had distinguished himself in the Polish campaign, winning an Iron Cross and promotion to sergeant (feldwebel). He had also fought in Crete, Tunisia, and Normandy, finally rising to oberfeldwebel, a first sergeant.

If Johannes Blaskowitz hoped to stop the Allies from overrunning the Army Group H sector and pouring into the industrial Ruhr, the field marshal would need to count on men like these two. Although Deutsch was an officer and Shafer an enlisted man, the pair treated each other as equals and with a mutual respect that was rare between a company commander and chief noncom.

"I would offer you a cigarette, Heinrich," Lieutenant Deutsch grinned, "but we have orders that there must be no light of any kind."

"I understand," Sergeant Shafer answered. He squinted into the silhouetted positions at Platte before he spoke again. "Herr Deutsch, do you believe the enemy truly intends to cross the Rhine in our sector?"

"I am certain of it," Deutsch answered. "The only question now is when and where they will attack."

"I suspect that one of their first targets will be to capture this very bridge on which we stand to control the railroad line."

"You are probably correct," the lieutenant nodded. "We may need to add more men on this bridge and perhaps set up more machine gun posts on either side."

"Do you believe we can stop them?"

"We stopped them at Arnhem," the A Company commander said. "They were superior to us in numbers, but we stopped them. If our resolve is strong enough, we will also stop them here."

"That was an airborne assault," Shafer said. "They jumped right into the barrels of our guns. Now, they will come after us on the ground, with tanks and mobile artillery leading the way."

"Perhaps so," the lieutenant nodded. "Even so, we will stop their ground assault as we did their parachute assault."

However, the two men from FJR 6 would get another opportunity to stop a new airborne assault. By late morning, hundreds of U.S. paratroopers would descend in their sector, men from the 17th Airborne's U.S. 513th Regiment: Lt. Col. Allen Miller, Capt. Harry Kenyon, Privates Stryker, Hines, Leonard, Walley, and hundreds of others. The Americans would drop from the sky in an attempt to gain the bridges and pikes of the Diersfordt railroad and parallel highway between Hamminkeln and Wesel.

Colonel Heydte, Lieutenant Deutsch, Sergeant Shafer and hundreds more from FJR 6 would find themselves in their harshest fight yet of the European war.

Finally, at dusk of 23 March, inside the battered city of Wesel itself, Col. Frederick Ross ambled amidst the devastated city to check his defenses. The Wesel Division commander had not been fooled by the Allied attempts to camouflage their movements eastward toward Wesel. The Allied aerial pounding of the communication centers at Hamminkeln and Dinslaken had all but exposed Montgomery's plan. Yet, while

Ross expected a water crossing of the Rhine, he had not guessed that the Allies had also planned an airborne drop north and east of Wesel.

The colonel had earlier finished a meal of simple sauerkraut and potatoes. He was still hungry as he surveyed his defenses along the northeast sector of Wesel where he found Capt. Wilhelm Geyer who commanded the makeshift Wesel Volkstrum Division's 2nd Battalion. This unit had taken up positions about the Issel Canal.

"Captain, are the men in place?"

"Yes, Herr Ross," Geyer answered, but an aura of uncertainty was on the captain's face.

The colonel could not help but notice this uneasiness. "We have reason to worry, Captain, for the enemy has countless aircraft, armor, and other equipment, while they can also muster millions of soldiers. Still, we have stopped them before and we can do so again."

"It is not the odds that I fear," Geyer said. "The Volkstrum troops are ill trained and inexperienced. This will be their first engagement in battle and they may panic and run."

The Volkstrum troops were only militia men, volunteers from their own local area who had in the past served mostly as supply troops, AA gunners, or air raid wardens. But with the loss of so many Wehrmacht regulars, they had been pressed into service. Most of them were elderly or young teenagers. Still, they understood the importance of holding this city.

"These men will fight," Ross assured Geyer. "Anyway, a cadre of experienced parachute troops will join us. A platoon of them will be assigned to your battalion, and I suggest you deploy them among your men with one squad to each company, and one squad in reserve."

"That is good news," Geyer said. "I will follow your suggestion when these paratroopers arrive."

"Have confidence," Ross tapped the captain on the shoulder. "We may yet hurl back our enemies. We have successfully destroyed all bridges crossing the Rhine, and we have stationed artillery units all along the banks to shell any boats that attempt to cross the river."

The colonel had barely finished speaking when Lt. Heinz Becker of the 7th Parachute Division interrupted the Wesel Division commander. "Please excuse my intrusion, sir. I am Lieutenant Becker of the 7th Parachute, and I was told to bring my platoon here to join this unit."

Colonel Ross grinned. "Ah, the cadre has arrived."

"Yes sir."

Ross nodded at the 2nd Battalion commander. "This is Capt. Wilhelm Geyer. He will instruct you on how he wants your men deployed."

Becker looked at the captain and bowed slightly. "Herr Geyer."

"I welcome you and your men," Geyer said.

Colonel Ross shuttled his glance between Geyer and Becker and then spoke again. "I will leave you now to check on other units. You two can discuss between yourselves how best to use the parachute platoon."

"Yes, Colonel," Captain Geyer said.

When the Wesel Division commander departed, Geyer turned to Becker, "Lieutenant, I know that the 7th Parachute Division has seen extensive combat. You will be of great service to us."

"We have seen our share of battle, Captain," Becker said. "But the enemy has been too strong and we now face a most dangerous peril. If the Allies break our defenses again, they can drive into the heart of our homeland."

"That is why we cannot falter," Geyer said.

Geyer took Becker through the 2nd Battalion defenses along the canal facing south. The captain expected the enemy to attempt landings not only directly against Wesel, but also to the south in an attempt to swing north and take the Issel waterway. Geyer had stationed two companies of men at the edge of the city on both the dams and canal locks, with at least a dozen machine gun nests, several mortar teams, and several 88mm artillery pieces. He hoped the mortar and artillery crews would destroy any Allied troops that forded the Rhine, skirted Wesel, and then tried to reach the Issel Canal. Geyer also left a company of similarly armed troops facing north.

Becker found the Volkstrum troops quite high in morale and intent on holding the city. These troops knew that the fall of Wesel would open the door to the industrial Ruhr. Dozens of towns and cities, thousands of civilians, and hundreds of factories could become victims of enemy hordes. These raw Volkstrum troops viewed these veteran paratroopers with awe and admiration and they eagerly sought their advice on how best to ready themselves against the enemy.

Lt. Heinz Becker deployed his men carefully, leaving one squad with each Volkstrum company and putting combat-tested sergeants in command of these companies. The feldwebels, in turn assigned three men to each company platoon, one to advise riflemen, one to direct machine gunners, and one to work with mortar teams. The paratroopers would make certain that Volkstrum troops knew where and how to hold, and when to retreat into secondary positions if they became overwhelmed by the enemy.

"You should study carefully the areas behind you," Lieutenant Becker told his sergeants, "so you can fall back and still find good secondary positions from which to defend yourselves. Make contingency plans for an orderly withdrawal if such withdrawals become necessary and you will suffer minimal losses in men and arms. If we can wear down the enemy and inflict heavy casualties on his units, we may force them to retire. We cannot hope to repel our enemies with mere fire power, for they are too strong. Only a wise strategy, exceptional cunning, and stalwart determination can defeat them."

The sergeants nodded.

"Most of all," Becker gestured, "you must instill faith in these raw soldiers by your own personal resolve and exemplary behavior under fire. If you do not panic and you do not falter, the Volkstrum soldiers will hold with you."

When Becker completed his instructions, he

ambled along the canal bank and stared into the silence to the east. Soon, Captain Geyer came next to him. "Have you finished your deployments?"

"Yes, Herr Geyer."

"Then all we can do now is wait." He then poked Becker gently. "We will hold, Lieutenant, we will hold them."

"Let us hope so."

In 12 hours, Geyer would know whether or not his battalion and its attached paratroopers could hold. However, he would not find infantrymen coming after him, but an enemy coming down in flimsy gliders, GIs from the 194th Regiment: Col. James Pierce, Capt. Fred Wittig, Sergeants Woolfort, Hedrick, Martin, Noldau, and a host of other glider troops who would skid into the areas north of the Issel Canal and attempt to capture the vital waterway.

CHAPTER FIVE

At 0100 hours, 24 March, 1944, the dense smoke screen still hung in the air over the Rhine River basin, dimming the three-quarter moon that now left a pale light on the surface of the river and a pastel glow on the silhouetted rubble of Wesel. The GIs waiting on the west bank stared at the obscured opposite bank. The smoke screen had billowed over the expected battle area since 1000 hours, three hours ago, fed by generators that released the mist. By now, the dense concentration of chemical pot had brought nausea to American troops. Many of the soldiers were coughing heavily and some had become quite ill, vomiting from the gaseous odor. Finally, Col. Branner Purdue, commander of the 513th Regiment, called the chemical battalion.

"You've got to shut down those generators," the colonel bellowed. "I'll have my whole regiment on sick call before we cross the river."

"We have orders to keep up the smoke all night, sir," somebody answered.

"Forget those orders," Purdue barked. "Turn off those generators."

"Yes sir."

East of Wesel, along the Lippe River and Momm River tributary, the troops of the 116th Panzer Division could see the heavy smoke screen above the Rhine, a thick mist that almost hit the black outlined ruins of Wesel. In the 60th Grenadier positions, Col. Walter Harzer walked among his entrenched troops, offering encouragement to hold their ground against any American attempt to capture the waterways. When he reached the 3rd Battalion lines, he spoke to Maj. Sepp Krafft.

"We can expect an attack by dawn, or even tonight," the colonel said. "If they bypass Wesel and attempt to take these bridges and then move on to Schanzenberg, your battalion must stop them."

"I understand," Krafft nodded.

"How many tanks do you have?"

"Seven medium tanks and five Tigers," the major answered. "Not many, but we will make good use of them."

"Good," the colonel said.

Inside Wesel itself, Col. Frederick Ross squinted through the chemical smoke. He saw nothing on the other side of the river, but he knew the Americans were there and that they would soon start crossing the Rhine.

"Achtung!" Ross quipped. "If they come, we will not even see them until they are on the river bank."

"That is unfortunate," his aide answered. "But we know they are coming and we will be ready. I have alerted the battalions to the north and west, and Captain Geyer assured me that his 2nd Battalion is in position. I can tell you honestly, Herr Ross, that the paratroopers have been invaluable. They have greatly bolstered the morale of our troops with their presence and their leadership. They will make a difference."

"Let us hope so," Ross said.

But as the Germans waited in their positions for the expected Allied assault, the eruption of countless artillery pieces from the west bank of the river suddenly shattered the nighttime silence. The Allies had opened their mammoth artillery barrage preparatory to the assault across the river. From the American sector, more than 1,000 guns lobbed an array of shells from 25 pounders to 350 pounders across the river. The shells exploded in numbing orange balls all along an eight mile front and several miles deep. Explosions erupted in and around Wesel, Mollen, Schanzenburg, Wickershamm, Dinslaken, and a dozen other towns and crossroads in between. German troops sheltered themselves in cellars, dugouts, or underground bunkers to wait out the horrendous cannonade. Wehrmacht soldiers along the river, canal, railroad, or highway positions burrowed themselves deep into trenches.

For more than an hour the thundering explosives shot across the Rhine. Bursting shells fell on numerous positions to kill dozens of German soldiers; or the shells brought down more of the rubble in Wesel and other towns; or the shellfire ripped up patches of roadways, damaged bridges, or chopped up sections of railroad pikes. However, the Germans had expected the cannonade and despite the numbing fire from these hundreds of guns, the Germans had not suffered as badly as the Allies had hoped.

Sgt. John Ramer had guessed right when he said that aerial and artillery assaults did not destroy the Germans; that "Those bastards are still fighting when we get there."

Not until 0200, 24 March, after the Allies had expended almost 65,000 rounds of shells, did the barrage finally lift. Smoke rose into the dark sky from an oblong of terrain some 20 miles long and several miles deep. Flickering fires also dotted the extensive patch of landscape. As soon as the cannonade ended, Branner Purdue, commander of the U.S. 120th Infantry Regiment, sent an order up and down the west bank.

"Move out! Move out!"

In G Company, Capt. Charles Moncrieff yelled to his platoon leaders and officers. "Okay, we're shoving off!"

In the LCIs, the GIs stiffened when the idling engines revved harder and the boats cleared the west shoreline. Pvt. Rex Anderson squinted into the now clearing smoke screen and studied the heavy palls of smoke beyond. Cpl. Les Belden stared up the sky, tightened the satchel bag about his waist, and then pushed his helmet harder on his head as the LCI bounced over the small waves on the river. Pvt. Earl Otto, one of the BAR men, sat rigidly with an aura of pride and rubbed his heavy automatic rifle. Sgt. John Ramer only sat stoically.

T/Sgt. Harry Boures, the 2nd Platoon leader, glanced at the men aboard the barge with a tingle of uneasiness. Many of his platoon infantrymen were replacements who had never been in combat before and he wondered if the young GIs might panic if they met enemy fire. The big, burly sergeant from Buffalo, N.Y., rubbed his dry lips and then squinted at the east bank. He almost cursed: one damn river after another ever since D-Day over nine months ago. Boures had been a mere corporal when he hit Omaha Beach. Three rivers later, beyond St. Lo, he had made Sergeant. Then had come the Risle River, the Seine beyond Paris, and the Muesse in Argonne. By the time he had crossed the Orr in Belgium, Boures was a tech sergeant and a platoon leader.

Two months after the nightmarish Battle of the Bulge, the burly sergeant was again crossing a river. The upstate New Yorker felt only one consolation this time—the Rhine was the last obstacle before marching into the heart of Germany. For the sake of the new men in his platoon, he hoped the artillery had done its job and G Company met little resistance.

Then a sudden bump jerked Boures from his

77

meditations. He heard the clanging sound of chains and the bow gangway fell from the LCI to the river bank. "Move it! Move it!" the harsh voice of Lt. Art Saalfield echoed along the river bank.

Boures looked at his watch: 0200 hours. He then gestured to his men. "Stay easy and stay alert." When the men scampered down the ramp to dry land, the sergeant turned to Corporal Belden. "Les, when we get organized, you take the point."

"Okay, Sarge," Belden said.

The twelve men from the barge loitered on the river bank, where they met no opposition, while Boures tried to find the rest of his platoon. However, a mere 36 men of G Company had reached the east bank and even some of these were separated. Only 24 men had landed with Lieutenant Saalfield and Sergeant Boures. The G Company exec searched for Captain Moncrieff and the others but they were nowhere in sight. The lieutenant only found the other twelve men of the company. Saalfield learned that the company had been separated and he called the men he had into a circle.

"G Company had all kinds of trouble coming across. We're the only ones here at check point."

"What?" Sergeant Ramer hissed.

The executive officer shook his head. "Our storm boats got scattered. Some of them broke down and went back to the west bank, and a few got stranded on some river islands. I don't know where the captain is."

"What the hell are we going to do, Lieutenant?" Boures asked.

"Our objective is this bridge and we're going after it."

"We're going to take a bridge with thirty-six men?" Boures huffed.

"That's why we crossed the Rhine," Saalfield answered sharply.

However, before the 36 men moved out, 20 G Company GIs straggled up to join the others. "Sorry," one of the newcomers said, "they landed us quite a ways from the check point."

"At least you're here and that'll help," Saalfield said. "Let's go."

"What about the rest of the battalion?" Boures asked.

"I'll check it out," Saalfield answered. He then called Lt. Col. Ed Cantey, who had personally mustered the other two companies of 2nd Battalion. "This is Ginger 8; Ginger 8 to Able Leader."

"Able Leader," Cantey said. "Where the hell are you?"

"We're at check point for our unit, sir."

"Okay, get to your Bill objective. We've already hit Mehrum and taken a few prisoners. You shouldn't run into much trouble. Let me speak to Captain Moncrieff."

"He's not here, sir. This is Lieutenant Saalfield. Our company got separated. I understand that some of the boats didn't make it across the river. I've only got fifty-six men."

"Son of a bitch," Cantey cursed. "Well, you'll have to push on with whatever you have."

"Yes sir."

"Call me when you've taken your objective."

"Will do, sir," Saalfield answered. He then turned to Boures. "Sergeant, take a dozen men ahead of us; we'll follow and cover in case of trouble."

"Yes sir."

Boures moved quickly ahead with twelve men, including squad leader John Ramer, Cpl. Les Belden, Pvt. Earl Otto, and Pvt. Rex Anderson. This forward unit pushed on swiftly for 1500 yards, passing the battered town of Mehrum that other units of 2nd Battalion had already secured. The platoon non-com came within 300 yards of the objective and then held up before he peered hard through his field glasses.

"What do you see, Harry?" Ramer asked.

"Nothing; not a goddamn thing."

"Maybe there's nobody there."

"Those krauts aren't going to abandon that bridge," Boures said. "We'll leave a machine gun team here and the rest of us will check out the target."

By the time Boures had set up the machine gun, Saalfield arrived with the rest of the men. "What's the holdup, Sergeant?"

"I've set up a machine gun to cover us."

"We've got to take that bridge in a hurry and then take the town of Schanzenberg on the other side. That's an important point. Move out. We'll follow. Anyway, I don't think there's anybody on that bridge. I think the Germans have run off."

But the Germans had not abandoned the

bridge. Maj. Sepp Krafft had been watching the approach of the 2nd Battalion GIs for more than an hour. He had been in contact with units of his battalion covering this defensive sector, including troops at Mehrum, Schanzenberg, Wurmgutterswich, and the Lippe River. He had learned that Mehrum had fallen and its defenders had retreated into Schanzenberg. Now, even as the GIs from G Company approached, Krafft received more distressing news from Colonel Harzer. The 60th Grenadier commander told the major that another large enemy force was closing on Gotterswickerham, a key town on the Lippe River.

"Sepp, you must hold the bridge; you must hold," Harzer said. "If the enemy takes the bridge, they can sweep into Schanzenberg and cut off our troops to the west."

"We will do our best, Colonel."

"Are the tanks ready?"

"I have most of them in Schanzenberg, with three of them forward," Major Krafft said. "Even now, we can see the enemy approaching the bridge, but we will have a strong greeting for them."

"Good, good," Harzer answered.

T/Sgt. Harry Boures, meanwhile, moved cautiously toward the span over the Lippe River. But within 250 yards, a sudden chatter of machine gun fire spewed across the dark terrain. Two GIs caught hits and fell prostrate. One man had his jaw torn off and another caught two heavy slugs in the chest that ripped open his torso. Two more men from Boures' unit suffered wounds, one from a hit in the leg and the other from a hit in the shoulder.

"Hit the dirt!" Boures cried.

The surviving men quickly dropped to the ground as the machine gun fire continued to chatter through the darkness.

"Son of a bitch!" the platoon sergeant cursed. He turned to Private Otto who was lying next to him. "Earl, we got to get that gun."

"How, Sarge?" Otto asked acidly.

Boures turned to Sergeant Ramer, who was also lying prostrate near the platoon sergeant. "Johnny, keep us covered." When Ramer nodded, Boures motioned to Otto. "Let's go." The two men crawled forward, snaking over the terrain and occasionally stopping to wince when another chatter of machine gun fire streamed over their heads. Finally, they came within 40 yards of the German machine gun nest. During a period of fleeting silence, Boures motioned to Otto. The private rose to his knees and unleashed a barrage of BAR fire at the nest. Fifty caliber slugs pinged off a defensive metal plate or ripped up sandbags, sending puffs of dust into the air. The fire momentarily drove the Germans to cover and Boures crept swiftly to the flank of the gun position before he flattened himself on the ground again.

The German machine gunners, unaware that Boures had come almost on top of them, continued to fire to the south. Otto felt terrified and helpless in his forward, isolated position and he hugged the ground while he held his helmet tightly on his head. But then the private heard a sudden b-bloom and looked up to see the nest erupt in fragments. Boures had obviously tossed a grenade right on target. Then Otto heard a cry from the platoon non-com.

"Let's go!"

Otto did not falter, nor did the others of the 2nd Platoon hesitate. Soon, the seven men joined Boures in the shattered machine gun pit where three Germans lay in grotesque, distorted death, victims of the grenades. Four more Germans came out of a ditch behind the nest with upraised hands to surrender.

"Komarad! Aufgeben! Aufgeben!"

Boures shoved the four soldiers ahead of him and then turned to Les Belden. "Take these prisoners to the rear. Tell the lieutenant he can move ahead, and tell him to send medics to take care of the wounded."

"Okay," Belden said.

Within a half hour, Saalfield and the G Company GIs continued toward the Lippe River bridge, but now they moved warily. The lieutenant often stopped to peer through field glasses, although he saw nothing ahead of him. However, the Germans were well camouflaged. When the Americans came within 100 yards of the bridge, raking machine gun fire from two nests ripped across the terrain. A half dozen dogfaces fell and the lieutenant cried frantically.

"Hit the dirt!"

While the men remained in their prostrated positions, Saalfield crawled among his troops to count casualties. Two more infantrymen had died from hits in the head and stomach respectively, and four injured squirmed painfully about the ground like wounded cougars. "Medic! Medic!" Saalfield cried.

Two men hurried forward and attended to the wounded before taking them to the rear. Then, Saalfield turned to Boures. "Sergeant, we've got those obstacles up ahead. Take some men and flank them." But then the officer and his GIs cowered as renewed machine gun fire rattled through the night. Saalfield looked soberly at Boures. "If we don't get those nests, they'll get us."

"Okay, Lieutenant."

Boures took three men with him, including BAR man Earl Otto, to hit one of the nests, and he sent Sgt. John Ramer to the right with three men to destroy the second machine gun position. The two small parties crawled cautiously forward, stopping and clawing into the earth whenever a new barrage of machine gun fire echoed through the darkness. Still, none of the eight men were hit and they finally came within range of the two gun posts. A moment later, the GIs lobbed grenades like rocks before a staccato of b-blooms erupted flaming bursts of light. Then, powdery dust and clodding chunks of earth settled to the ground while a silence prevailed within the two German emplacements.

Harry Boures lifted his head carefully and squinted at the battered positions. He saw no movement and he heard no sounds, so he ges-

84

tured to his men. Soon, the octet reached the nests where they found only dead, bloodied German soldiers. Boures jumped into one of the pits and he coughed from the smell of grenade smoke that still wisped about the area. Then as he looked at the silhouetted shapes on the Lippe River bridge, John Ramer came next to him.

"For Christ sake, Harry, how many more of these nests do we have between here and that bridge?"

"I don't know," Boures shook his head.

"The bastards," Ramer cursed. "After all that aerial and artillery bombardment, those krauts are still alive, kicking, and waitin' for us. What do we do now?"

"Wait for the lieutenant," Boures said.

Maj. Sepp Krafft, on the Lippe River bridge, had heard the heavy exchange of fire and grenade explosions, but he did not know what had happened. As a precaution, Krafft ordered two burp gun soldiers to bolster the machine gun teams at the foot of the bridge. He also directed one of the big Tiger tanks onto the bridge, with its 88mm gun pointing southward. Krafft peered through his field glasses. In the heavy darkness, however, he could not see the Americans. Still, he would be ready for them if or when they approached the bridge.

While Krafft reinforced his defenses, Lieutenant Saalfield studied the bridge again through field glasses and he saw the black shapes near the base. He rightly suspected that the shadows were enemy soldiers who were manning still more machine guns. He turned to his 2nd Platoon non-com. "Sergeant, more bad news. I think they've got more nests up ahead. We'll need to clear them."

"Lieutenant, I don't think we should get that close. They'll spot us for sure from the deck of the bridge and shoot us up good. I suggest we knock out those nests with mortar fire."

"Okay," Saalfield nodded. He picked up his walkie talkie and called Lieutenant Colonel Cantey. "This is Ginger 8; we need a mortar team."

"Where the hell are you, Ginger 8?" Cantey growled.

"About a hundred yards from Objective Bill. We've taken out three machine gun nests so far, but there's a couple more at the foot of our target. If we get too close to them, they'll get us from the bridge."

"We can't wreck that bridge," the 2nd Battalion commander said. "We need it intact for use by armored vehicles."

"Sir," Saalfield insisted, "if we don't knock out those machine gun nests, we can't take that bridge, and we can't do it without mortar. As I said, we're too close and enemy troops will spot us and cut us apart."

"Okay," Cantey said. "Hold your positions and I'll get a mortar team to you."

Nearly an hour passed and during the silence the GIs remained put while the Germans guarding the bridge awaited the Americans' next move. Finally, a 51mm mortar team arrived and Saalfield ordered an attack on the two silhouetted areas up ahead. The mortar men quickly assembled their weapons and then the sergeant looked at the lieutenant. "Sir, we'll be cutting this awfully close. I can't promise we won't damage the bridge."

"I don't care," Saalfield said, "I've lost enough men and I'm not losing anymore because of that goddamn bridge."

"Yes sir."

The mortar team proved quite adept. At 0500 hours, just before dawn, a thumping mortar shell landed almost squarely on the first German gun position. The resulting explosion tore the position to shreds, leaving only debris and dead Germans. The next mortar shell near missed the second machine gun nest, but the third shell came much closer, killing two members of the German team and wounding two others. The injured Germans scrambled out of the wrecked nest, bloody and hurt, and staggered toward the bridge.

"Nice job, Sergeant," Saalfield grinned at the mortar team leader. Then he turned to his men. "Okay, let's go, but watch yourselves. We don't know what they've got on the bridge itself."

On the span, Maj. Sepp Krafft peered once more through his field glasses and now, even in the dark, he could see the dark shapes crawling toward the bridge. The German major gestured and the Mark V suddenly ignited its engine and growled forward, vibrating the steel deck of the 60 foot long span. Inside the armored vehicle, the tank leader swung the big 88mm barrel and locked the gun on the G Company solders.

Beyond the bridge, when the Americans heard the rumble, they stopped and stiffened. Men like Saalfield, Boures, Ramer, and other combat veterans clearly recognized the sound of the Mark tank. They had run into them before—in the Ruhr Valley, in the Bulge, in France, and in the hedgerows of Normandy. Soon, the Americans saw the ugly muzzle on the bridge loom out of the darkness.

Saalfield gaped for a moment and then cried sharply. "Scatter!"

Just as the GIs dispersed, Major Krafft dropped his arm. "Fire!"

The first barking 88 shell roared out of the Tiger's gun barrel and exploded in the midst of the GIs. The burst killed three Americans outright and wounded three more. Seconds later, another bark from the Mark V sent another concussioning explosion into the Americans, killing another two men and wounding four more. Luckily, before the third shell struck the G Company ranks, the GIs had dived into craters, ravines, or smashed German machinegun positions. But here they cowered—terrified and seemingly trapped.

In one hole, Lt. Art Saalfield crouched next to Sgt. John Ramer, Pvt. Rex Anderson, Cpl. Les Belden, and the company radio man. In a nearby hole were Pvt. Earl Otto, and two other GIs. The octet, like other cowering Americans, remained silent and tense, unable to move, and wondering if the next 88mm shell would blow them to oblivion. Finally Saalfield called Lieutenant Colonel Cantey.

"This is Ginger 8; Ginger 8."

"We read you."

"A tank, sir, a big Tiger sitting right in the middle of the bridge. That monster has already killed or maimed a dozen of my men. We can't move. We need help to knock it out."

"We can't destroy that bridge," Cantey said.

"Sir, there's no way we can get across that bridge with that tank in front of us."

"We've got to have that bridge intact," Lieutenant Colonel Cantey insisted, "and we've got to take that town on the other side. Schanzenberg is a road center and the krauts may start pouring reinforcements in there by daylight. I'll send up F Company to help out. Maybe we can get the tank with bazookas."

"That Mark V's 88mm gun will cut bazooka men to pieces before they get close enough for a shot."

"Lieutenant," Cantey said again, "it's vital that we take that bridge intact. We've got armor, TDs, and artillery moving up fast now. We need the span to get this heavy stuff across the Lippe River. We don't have time to lay Bailey bridges or even a pontoon bridge across the Lippe. Hold your position and wait for F Company. Captain Jackson will take over your operation to capture the bridge and the town beyond."

"Yes sir," Saalfield said.

The G Company soldiers remained in their holes while the Mark tank occasionally loosed

89

another 88mm shell that chopped new craters into the terrain beyond the bridge; or the tank intermittently fired a staccato of machine gun fire. For nearly 15 minutes, the German tank crew continued its on and off action, just enough to keep the Americans pinned down.

Each passing moment heightened Saalfield's anxiety. Daylight would emerge in another half hour and his GIs would be totally exposed. The tank could then cut his men to pieces. Private Anderson saw the anxiety on the lieutenant's face and he too understood the peril that would come with daylight. Then, he looked at the bag around Belden's waist — explosives,

"Les," Anderson said, "can you work up a satchel charge?"

Belden frowned. "Sure, but —"

"Maybe we can place one on that tank."

The corporal's eyes widened and he rolled a tongue around his lips. He did not speak and Anderson looked at the executive officer. "Sir, we've got to try it, or we'll all be dead come daylight."

Sergeant Ramer stared in astonishment at Anderson's proposal, but Saalfield rubbed his chin, studied Anderson intently, and then looked at Belden. "Corporal, I would not order you to do anything like that. But I have to agree with Anderson. If we don't take out that tank before daybreak, they could chop us to pieces. If we do take out the tank, we can probably take the bridge intact."

Belden shuttled his glance among the lieutenant, the private, and the sergeant who shared his shelter. Then he grinned. "It's like Anderson says, sir. If we don't do something, we'll all be dead by sunup."

Lt. Art Saalfield nodded, but an agony boiled in his stomach.

CHAPTER SIX

Lt. Art Saalfield watched soberly as Belden and Anderson worked from material in the corporal's kit to fashion a jelly satchel charge. Saalfield even ignored the occasional 88mm shells that still exploded in numbing concussions or the infrequent chatter of machine guns that spewed over the open terrain south of the Lippe River bridge. Finally, the two GIs were ready and Belden looked at the officer.

"We're ready, Lieutenant."

Saalfield nodded and looked at Ramer. "We'll cover them from here."

The squad sergeant, still numb from this proposed attempt to get the tank, did not even react. The lieutenant then called to Harry Boures who was in the crater next to him. "Sergeant, Corporal Belden and Private Anderson are going after that tank with a satchel charge. Notify as many men as you can to cover them."

Boures' eyes widened and his mouth fell open. The platoon sergeant could not believe that these two men could reach the Tiger. He feared that machine gun fire would riddle them before they got within 50 feet of the Mark V. Still, like Saalfield, Boures also saw the value of knocking out this tank before daylight when the armored monster could eliminate the G Company GIs. Boures rolled his tongue around his lips and then answered.

"Okay, Lieutenant, we'll do what we can."

Then Boures and the others of G Company watched the two GIs crawl out of their holes and slither across the terrain like huge roaches, Anderson dragging a Thompson submachine gun and Belden dragging his satchel bag. Boures saw the two men move northeast, away from the bridge, until they reached the river bank. The sergeant then cowered from a new chatter of machine gun fire that spewed out of the tank, almost directly south. The fire actually brightened Boures' hopes: Belden and Anderson had not yet been detected.

Meanwhile, the two GIs wiggled along the river bank and soon reached one of the bridge piers. They squinted upward, but saw no one on the span. Apparently, the Germans were content to leave the 50 ton tank as guardian of the structure. Belden gestured to Anderson before both men shimmied up the side of the pier and then across the undertrusses of the bridge. Finally, they reached a point squarely opposite the right lateral of the Mark V. The two men cautiously peered left and right. Anderson saw a few dark figures to the left, Germans at the north end of the bridge. He turned to Belden.

"Do you think you can plant that charge before they spot us?"

"Can you keep me covered?" Belden whispered back.

The private nodded and then scrambled up to the bridge deck and crouched tightly against the side of the tank before he gestured to Belden. The corporal hurried onto the deck himself and quickly extracted the satchel charge from his bag. He pressed the jelly explosive tightly against the turret joint, the most vulnerable point on a Mark V. Then he adhered a fuse to it.

"Okay, let's go," Belden said in a hoarse whisper.

But before the pair could leave the bridge, the figures on the north end saw the two GIs. A volley of rifle fire erupted and the German soldiers hurried forward. Anderson opened with his submachine gun and dropped two of the Germans before the others flattened themselves on the bridge deck.

"We've got to get out of here," Anderson cried. "You go first. I'll cover."

Belden looked at the burning fuse and then flipped himself off the bridge deck and onto the underpinning of the truss. Anderson glanced at Belden and then turned to loose another barrage of automatic fire before he started for the truss himself. However, a heavy chatter from a burp gun put three bullets into the private's chest and stomach, erupting sudden gushes of blood. Anderson wobbled a few feet and then toppled off the bridge and plopped into the Lippe River below.

Belden stared down in shock as his companion disappeared under the water. Then he turned his head quickly when he heard the cries of men, the heavy thud of boots, and the crack of rifle fire. He let go of the bridge and dropped into the river, hoping to swim to safety.

Four German soldiers came next to the tank and peered down at the river with aimed weapons. They would open on Belden as soon as he surfaced. But an explosion erupted on the bridge at the exact moment that Belden's head popped above the water. The blast smacked the four German soldiers with heavy chunks of metal flying off the bursting tank, killing two of them instantly and badly wounding the other pair. The same blast tore apart the guts of the Mark V that burst into flames. Cries of anguish erupted from within the Tiger and two burning men, all who survived, pushed open the hatch and scrambled out of the tank.

As the conflagration roared in and about the tank, Lt. Art Saalfield rose to his feet, stared in awe at the flames momentarily, and then gestured to his men. "Okay, move out! Let's get on that bridge!"

The G Company troops did not hesitate. They

scrambled out of their holes and rushed forward toward the bridge. Sgt. John Ramer peered intently, amazed that the two GIs had pulled off this feat. S/Sgt. Harry Boures merely stared in astonishment at the burning tank, and Pvt. Earl Otto looked at the fire in disbelief. Within a few minutes, the GIs reached the bridge and moved cautiously forward from both sides. When a sudden stream of fire came from the north end, the Americans ducked behind the burning Mark V, an excellent shelter. Then Otto moved carefully forward with his BAR and fired furiously, sending the German defenders scurrying for cover.

Meanwhile, Boures quickly set up two machine guns and moments later the gunners spewed heavy .50 caliber fire into the north end of the bridge. At least a half dozen more Germans fell from the withering fire, enabling the GIs to rush forward in safety. Sergeant Boures' unit reached the north end quickly where he found a dozen dead Germans and six more with upraised hands.

"Aufgeben! Aufgeben!"

Boures lowered his Thompson and then gestured to those who came after him. "Take these krauts to the rear."

A moment later, Lieutenant Saalfield had also reached the north end of the bridge. He surveyed the now abandoned German guns in front of him. "Sergeant," he told Boures, "they've obviously retreated into Schanzenberg. We'll set up machine gun posts here in case they try a counterattack. We'll hold until Captain Jacobsen gets here with F Company."

"Yes sir."

By daylight, Cpl. Les Belden had reached the bridge and although dripping wet he reported immediately to Saalfield. "Rex did a good job covering me, sir, but he got hit just as we were trying to get away. His body is in the river."

"I'm sorry, Corporal."

"Yeh," Belden nodded with a tinge of bitterness.

Only a few moments later, the GIs of F Company reached the bridge, and a half hour later, the remnants of G Company, about 100 men under Capt. Charles Moncrieff, also reached the bridge. Moncrieff stared at the wrecked tank and the wisps of smoke that still rose from the charred vehicle. He looked at Saalfield with an admiring grin

"Goddamn, Art, what a job. You and your men did one hell of a job."

"Yes, sir."

"We got scattered all over the goddamned river during the crossing," Moncrieff continued, "but we're here now. We'll muster our troops and join F Company to take that town," he cocked his head toward Schanzenberg. "We can't let them stage any troops there."

"No, sir," Saalfield said.

Captain Moncrieff called the 2nd Battalion commander. "This is Ginger 8. Please come in, Able Leader."

"Able Leader here," Lieutenant Colonel Cantey answered.

"We've taken Target Bill intact and we're getting ready to move into Target Abner."

"Good," the 2nd Battalion commander answered. He told Moncrieff that Company E and Company H had secured Mehrum. The two companies, under Lieutenant Colonel Cantey himself, were now moving into the next objective, Lohnen on the Lippe River. Once they secured this second target, they would be ready to cross the river and cut the railroad and highway that ran along the Lippe into Wesel. It was imperative that G Company and F Company now take Schanzenberg.

Meanwhile, the 3rd Battalion of the 120th Regiment had crossed the Rhine about 0330 hours and seized the small town of Ettroig by 0425 hours with the support of a heavy weapons platoon of mortar and small 37mm portable artillery. The 3rd had then moved swiftly toward Wickershamm, a town lying on a rise above a dike on the shore of the Lippe River. The town had appeared a formidable stronghold, with German gun positions commanding the approaches.

Still, Maj. Chris McCollough, the 3rd Battalion commander, had pressed on his men and weathered the sporadic artillery fire from Wickershamm. Fortunately, the German unit, another battalion from the 116th Panzer Division, had a limited number of shells and they had used their artillery sparingly. As the U.S. 3rd Battalion troops neared the town, the Germans fired 88mm shells from several tanks within the town. Mc-

Collough then waited until a full battery of artillery came up to his positions to unleash a barrage of fire. The heavy U.S. cannonade destroyed some of the positions and even knocked out two of the tanks.

By daylight, the heavy American artillery had forced the Germans to retire, and by 0600 hours, lead elements of McCollough's battalion had crossed the Lippe River and entered the southern outskirts of the town. Engineers quickly laid a pontoon bridge across the narrow river before American tank destroyers barreled into town, dragging heavy artillery after them.

Throughout the remainder of the morning, the 3rd would clear the town and open a road to the main highway and railroad pike that ran westward into Wesel. Once secured, the Americans would cut off the Lippe River route to reinforce the Wesel defenders.

While McCollough's 3rd Battalion moved relentlessly forward on the Wickershamm sector, Capt. Charles Moncrieff prepared to move on Schanzenberg. Lieutenant Colonel Cantey had placed Moncrieff in charge of the combined G and F Companies since he was senior to Captain Jacobson. Moncrieff planned to send two platoons of F Company toward the town from the right, while he personally led the G Company GIs on the left.

"We've got some TDs from the 823rd Anti-Tank Battalion coming up to you," Cantey told Moncrieff. "They can support you on Target Abner. Wait for them and have your men use them for cover."

"Yes, sir."

Within a half hour, some twenty TDs had reached the captured Lippe River bridge to join Moncrieff's soldiers. The captain gestured to his men and they crouched cautiously behind the TDs, whose small 37mm guns pointed straight north into Schanzenberg. The Americans moved forward for nearly a half hour, with the first rays of the sun now rising from the east. Moncrieff had yet to receive fire from the town and he hoped that perhaps Target Abner had been abandoned and he might capture the objective without difficulty.

But the Germans were waiting.

Maj. Sepp Krafft, whose own 2nd Battalion troops had taken a beating at the Lippe River bridge, had withdrawn the remainder of his forces into Schanzenberg. Krafft still had the bulk of his Mark IV and Mark V tanks, along with a dozen small and a dozen large artillery pieces. The major stood in one of the battered buildings and peered through his field glasses at the approaching TDs. His own grenadiers waited anxiously for the order to fire, but Krafft waited until the Americans had come within 300 yards of Schanzenberg before he gave the sharp order.

A half dozen artillery pieces suddenly opened with heavy shells against the Americans, and the GIs scattered. However, erupting balls of fire killed several U.S. soldiers, tearing open torsos, decapitating heads, shearing off arms or legs, or ripping out intestines. The dead American soldiers lay like broken, contorted dolls, while some of the wounded staggered about in a daze, blood saturating their green fatigue uniforms or their stunned faces. Two of the TDs burst into flames from the same artillery fire and their crews tumbled out of the vehicles, screaming in pain from the enveloping fire.

Most of the GIs dove into craters recently gouged from the earth by German shells. The TDs of the 823rd Battalion zigzagged frantically about the open ground before the town of Schanzenberg, but two more of the armored vehicles caught direct artillery hits and burst into flames, searing to death the men inside.

Then suddenly, the Mark Vs opened with deadly 88mm guns, while the German tank crews also sent rattling machine gun fire into the ranks of the GIs. The tanks knocked out two more TDs and damaged another pair of tank destroyers, while 88mm shell chopped out more chunks of earth from the soft spring ground. Two shells hit an occupied crater squarely and riddled the cowering GIs with heavy, numbing shrapnel that killed the men instantly. And soon, some of the Tigers from the 116th Panzer rumbled over the rubbled streets, coming toward the Americans.

Captain Moncrieff stared in horror. They could not withdraw to the Lippe River bridge before the Mark Vs slew half of the combined G and F Company personnel. The G Company commander cursed. They had come across the Rhine with ten times the number of men, arms, guns, and ammo as had their German opponents. Last night, some 2,000 American guns had sent thousands of rounds of artillery shells into the gun positions, and all during the day yesterday, 600 heavy bombers, 400 medium bombers, and assorted fighter-bombers of the U.S. 9th Air Force had dropped 3,200 tons of bombs on the Army Group H defenses. Yet Moncrieff now found himself and his men facing imminent destruction from these German Tigers.

Allied tanks, more than 2,500 of them from several armored divisions, had not yet caught up to the plodding infantrymen. So, ironically, dogfaces like these men of G and F Companies still had no heavy armor support.

However, the Americans did have a trump card—the 9th Air Force fighter-bombers that now hovered above the Rhine River battle zone to offer air support wherever necessary. Moncrieff quickly called Lieutenant Colonel Cantey.

"Able, this is Ginger 8. We've got about a half dozen Tigers and a battery of artillery hitting us hard. We need air support in a hurry."

"Give me your coordinates."

"61.4 by 61.6," Moncrieff answered.

"I'll call liaison and get some air units to you on the double."

Fortunately, Moncrieff did not wait long. Only two minutes after he called, and before the German Mark Vs cleared Schanzenberg, two squadrons of fighter-bombers from the 354th Fighter Group roared toward the coordinate position. 32 Thunderbolts under Col. George Bickel had been in CAP over the Rhine since dawn, ready to support whichever ground units needed them. When Bickel got the call from the 30th Division liaison, he quickly called his pilots.

"We got a job about six miles east of Wesel. Coordinate is 61.4. A bunch of Mark Vs are working over some dogfaces. We'll attack in pairs. In pairs."

"We read you, Colonel," Maj. Jim Howard of the 321st Squadron said.

The cowering, frightened GIs soon heard the heavy whine of aircraft and then watched the P-47s roar low, in pairs, over the Lippe River bridge. Bickel, leading the aerial formation, unleashed a half dozen 5" rockets at the rumbling German tanks. Four of them missed, but struck the lead Mark V squarely and the Tiger burst into flames. Other pilots followed Bickel, unleashing more whooshing rockets and chattering machine gun fire. Within the next several minutes, three more of the tanks burst into flames and the others retreated, zigzagging back into the rubble of Schanzenberg.

However, Colonel Bickel was not finished. He arched his squadron about and then zoomed into the town to unleash more whooshing rocket fire and machine gun bursts. The second assault knocked out a half dozen German artillery positions and scattered 116th Panzer soldiers in a dozen directions. Then Bickel called Captain Moncrieff.

"This is A-20 support, Ginger 8. What else do you want?"

"Can you stay upstairs until we secure the

town?" Moncrieff asked.

"Will do, Ginger 8 — unless they call us somewhere else," Colonel Bickel said. "Make your move fast. Maybe you can overrun the place before those krauts get themselves reorganized."

The G Company commander thanked Bickel and then ordered an assault on Schanzenberg. The GIs scrambled out of their craters and holes and moved forward, again behind the TDs. This time, no heavy artillery or tank fire challenged them. They had come well inside the town before machine gun fire dropped a point man and a second GI from 2nd Platoon. Sgt. Harry Boures shouted.

"Take cover!"

As the men scrambled to shelter themselves behind rubble, Cpl. Les Belden stared in horror at the two wounded GIs, bleeding and moaning, and lying in the open. He handed his weapon to a fellow soldier and then hurried from his shelter to zigzag toward the two wounded men. A chatter of machine gun fire erupted countless pops of earth about him, and two 88mm shells shattered some of the rubble to his left. But Belden only crouched and wiggled on to his fallen comrades.

"You're crazy." the bleeding point man said to Belden.

"Shut up," the corporal answered. He then hoisted the GI on his shoulder and zigzagged away from the machine gun fire that peppered the rubbled street behind him. After Belden had safely deposited the point man, he went quickly back to get the second wounded man. This time, he put the man on his back, held him in an arm lock, and crawled back to the battered wall of a building behind which many of the 2nd Platoon GIs had sheltered themselves.

"Son of a bitch, you did it!" Boures grinned at Belden. "You're gonna get so many goddamn medals, you'll need an extra uniform to pin them on."

"You better call the medics, Sarge."

"Sure," the platoon leader answered.

Meanwhile, Captain Moncrieff peered through his field glasses to locate the positions of the German machine guns and 88mm artillery. He detected the nest in one of the cragged, but still standing buildings, and he spotted the tank with an 88mm muzzle just behind a wall. The captain looked up to see the P-47s still circling overhead.

"This is Ginger 8 to A-2 support; can you help us out again?"

"Where's the target, Ginger 8?"

Moncrieff studied his map and spoke again. "Coordinates 63.2."

"Hang on, Ginger 8," Colonel Bickel said.

A moment later, a trio of P-47s zoomed into Schanzenberg once more and in single file they unleashed heavy rocket fire into the building and wall. The subsequent explosions blew out the side of the structure and the German machine gun team. Other rockets ignited the half hidden Mark V.

"Okay, let's move," Moncrieff gestured.

As the American TDs again rumbled ahead,

the GIs followed behind. Maj. Sepp Krafft peered at the oncoming enemy through field glasses and scowled. He had already lost the Lippe River bridge, and other elements of American troops had stormed into Wickershamm on the Lippe River against another battalion from the 60th Grenadier Regiment. Now, this U.S. unit was decimating Krafft's battalion. Krafft had lost many of his tanks, half of his artillery, and more than 100 men killed or wounded. Further, the P-47s hung in the sky like predatory hawks waiting to pounce on him again.

Krafft agonized over his dilemma. He knew the vital importance of holding Schanzenberg, but he wondered how he could do so against the increasing American strength that had continually crossed the Rhine since the wee hours of the morning. Still, he must make the effort and he called on his Panzer grenadiers to take up positions inside the battered buildings for house to house combat.

"We must hold at all costs," Krafft said.

"Yes, Herr Major," one of the subordinates said, but there was little enthusiasm in his voice.

The German officer had reason to feel doubt, for the Americans were now determined. Lieutenant Saalfield led a platoon of men against one clump of buildings where Germans sent sniper fire toward the U.S. troops. Saalfield directed bazooka men who thumped shells into the paneless windows, tearing out walls and the sniping Germans inside. Within a half hour, Saalfield's platoon had killed more than a dozen Germans and taken 40 prisoners.

Down another street in battered Schanzenberg, Sgt. Harry Boures led half of his platoon against more resisting Germans in more battered buildings. Rifle fire whizzed from the windows at the zigzagging, crouching GIs. The platoon leader called on two heavy weapons men who carried the new portable 55mm rifle cannon that weighed only 45 pounds.

"Wherever you see rifle fire, let 'em have it," Boures said.

In building after building, the heavy weapons men sent 55mm shells into the open windows to blow out clumps of walls, windows, and German soldiers. Other GIs ducked into rubbled buildings and stormed into rooms, cellars, or upstairs chambers. They killed more Germans or forced more of them into surrender. Within an hour, Boures and his team of 20 men had cleansed an entire street, slaying more than 30 Germans and taking nearly 50 prisoners.

The Germans were fighting, but they no longer offered the diehard resistance that had once been the trademark of the elite Panzer grenadiers. They now surrendered in droves rather than die uselessly in a lost cause.

Up still another street, Sgt. John Ramer led a dozen men in house to house searches for German defenders. Ramer's team met only sporadic fire from some of the buildings and he too called on heavy weapons men to snuff out resistance with thumping 55mm shells. Ramer's squad had almost reached the end of a street when an 88mm shell landed to the left of the plodding dogfaces, exploded in a numbing concussion and killed five men in Ramer's squad. The sergeant and his survivors looked about in shock and then stared in horror at the growling Mark V that was bearing down on them. There was nowhere to run and nowhere to hide as the ugly 88mm barrel swung left and right.

Ramer looked at his GIs and then picked up a 55mm portable gun from one of the dead heavy weapons men. "Run for cover!"

"Where? There's no place to run."

Ramer scowled and the rail-thin sergeant turned and weaved forward with the heavy weapon toward the Tiger. A rattling spew of machine gun fire came from the Mark V's front aperture. One bullet struck the sergeant in the arm, another bullet struck him in the chest, and a third hit him in the stomach. Ramer staggered, but did not fall. He came within 15 yards of the tank and unleashed a 55mm shell that struck squarely and set the tank afire. The Mark V stopped dead in its tracks and burning bodies scrambled out of the hatch.

Ramer tried to raise the weapon again, but he had been shot to ribbons. He simply collapsed to the ground in his own pool of blood. The GIs, utterly astonished by Ramer's efforts, moved slowly forward and peered down at their dead, bloodied squad leader.

"Goddamn it," one of the soldiers hissed. "Did you ever see anything like that? Ever?"

The others did not answer. They just stared at

the fallen John Ramer, who would be awarded a posthumous DSC for his valiant effort.

For another hour, GIs of G and F Companies continued to clear Germans from the town. Finally, at 0900 hours, Maj. Sepp Krafft rubbed his face to temper his agony. He knew that Schanzenberg was lost and he would only lose more men for no purpose if he continued to fight. He turned to his battalion executive officer.

"We will retire to Hunxe."

"Yes, Herr Major."

Moments later, the remnants of Krafft's 2nd Battalion left their positions and hurried westward out of the battered town, scurrying swiftly toward the town of Hunxe. Ironically, other units of the 60th Grenadiers had also fled eastward to Hunxe, with Col. Walter Harzer himself leading the flight. The colonel would set up new positions either here or at Kirchhellen.

By 0915, Capt. Charles Moncrieff had secured Schanzenberg and he now looked north at the Lippe River tributary

"What do we do now, Captain?" Lieutenant Saalfield asked.

"I don't know," the captain shrugged. "Call battalion."

"Yes, sir," Saalfield answered.

CHAPTER SEVEN

At 0900 hours, 24 March, a skytrain of aircraft over two miles long hung over Belgium. 226 C-47s, 72 C-46s, and 453 C-47s towing 906 gliders carried the troops of the U.S. 17th Airborne Division. To the left of these formations, 42 C-54s, 752 C-47s, and 420 gliders carried the Tommies of the British 6th Airborne Division. Above and around this train were 676 American fighter planes and 213 RAF fighter planes to escort them. The fighters banked and arced and flitted about the sky on all sides of the C-46s, C-47s, and CG-4 gliders.

In the lead C-46 of the 513th Regiment, Col. Jim Coutts looked out a waist window. He could see above and beyond him swarms of fellow Commando transport planes that seemingly dangled in midair. Coutts' ears were almost numb from the steady drone of transport engines. The unusually warm days and bright sunshine had prevailed for the past eleven days, however, so Coutts considered this 24 March morning a perfect day for a jump. The ground would probably be firm and dry.

The colonel checked the steel flaps of his jump helmet and then yanked the flak jacket under his parachute straps. He then looked at his watch: 0935. They had only been airborne for a half hour, but the flight to the drop zone had already become monotonous. He craned his neck, while he squinted again out of the window for a sign of the drop area some five miles northeast of Wesel. Coutts would be the first man out among the nearly 8,000 men of the U.S. 17th Airborne Division's two paratroop regiments that would jump across the Rhine to seize the vital highway and railroad running from Hamminkeln to Wesel.

Seated on one of the hard seats of the C-46 along with Coutts were Maj. Paul Smith, commander of the 1st Battalion, several more officers, and a few enlisted men, including Pvt. George Peters. The private squirmed on his seat uneasily amidst this plane load of brass, and he crouched in a corner to keep his rangy body as inconspicuous as possible. He felt more uncomfortable with the presence of these VIPs around him than he did with the thoughts of the upcoming jump. He did not even speak to the few privates next to him.

Peters jerked when the deep voice of Colonel

Coutts boomed through the interior of the plane: "IP in ten minutes. Prepare for jump."

Now Peters reacted as did others aboard the Commando. He checked his gear: helmet, flak suit, parachute straps, weapons, and boots. For the next few minutes, the clang, tinkle, and ring of paraphernalia echoed through the interior of the C-46. Then the men stiffened, everybody from Peters to Coutts, as the jump sergeant opened the fuselage door of the Commando and positioned himself before the wide portal. The jump would come soon.

In another formation of planes to the east, Lt. Col. Allen Miller, CO of 2nd Battalion, 513th Regiment, looked out of the window of his C-46 transport plane and studied the array of accompanying aircraft in the droning unit of aircraft. As far as he could see, C-46s and C-47s hung in the sky, with some planes droning quite close to each other, too close, Miller thought. What if his own aircraft locked wings with the plane next to him? They might both go down. The lieutenant colonel half scowled, wrinkling his round face. Then he straightened his squat, 5'4" bull-like frame and stared at the 23 fellow paratroopers inside the plane with him. They were sitting on the hard metal seats with cold and sober faces.

Miller knew his men were tense, not because this would be their first combat jump, but because they feared the Germans. These men had faced the enemy before during the Bulge, the Huertgen, and the Roer Valley. For months, the brass had assured them the Germans were demoralized and finished, without arms, without an airforce, and with only a shell of its former army. But the men of the 513th had learned differently during their harsh fights with this tenacious enemy. The men expected the same stiff opposition now.

Allen Miller tilted his helmet that almost hung down to his ears. Then he fingered the parachute belt on his chest before he tugged at the top of his jump boots that almost reached his knees. The 2nd Battalion commander's helmet always came down quite far on his head and his boots always came far up his short legs. So the men called him "Boots and Helmet."

On the starboard side of the C-46, Capt. Oscar Fodder, the battalion surgeon, checked his medical kits and then stared out of the window to study the C-47s and C-46s that covered the sky as far as he could see. The surgeon grew tenser as they neared the drop zone as did others aboard the plane.

Some of the troopers on this C-46 looked at their watches and stiffened as they flew ever closer to IP. At their briefings that morning, they had heard the reports: massive artillery barrages had smashed most of the enemy positions, and heavy air bombardments had finished off what few Germans were left. The troopers would find little resistance on the east bank of the Rhine near and about the Wesel area.

But like the paratroops of other 513th Regiment battalions, these men of the 2nd Battalion also knew the exaggeration of such confident words. Airborne troops had been told the same thing before the jumps into Normandy on D-Day and the jumps into Holland during Operation Market Garden.

Miller's troops sat quietly and soberly on the hard seats. They occasionally looked at the hook-up man who stood near the door of the C-46 and his presence reminded the GIs that they would be jumping soon. Some of the men glanced out of the windows to look at the long straight columns of fellow Commandos and C-47 Gooney Birds that carried supplies and arms as well as men. Now and then, the troopers heard or saw a fighter plane zoom over the C-46. Some of the soldiers tried to sleep or they took dramamine pills to mitigate the nauseous feeling in their stomachs, a nausea nourished more from fear than air sickness.

Miller and his battalion would jump north of Wesel to seize the railroad line and set up defenses against any German infantry or Panzer units that tried to come down from the north or over from the east. They would leap just ahead of the 507th troops who would drop about three miles to the west of the 513th on the other side of the strategic woods around Diersfordt. Here, the 507th would take the town and the highway that ran southward to Wesel.

In E Company's C-46 of the 513th Infantry Regiment, the paratroopers appeared more relaxed, perhaps because most of the 24 men aboard were privates or PFCs. The highest rank aboard was Capt. Harry Kenyon, the company commander, and Lt. Dave McGuire, the executive officer. The men ignored the drone of engines or the hordes of fellow C-46s alongside of them.

For Pvt. Walt Leonard, Pvt. Paul Hines, Pvt. Stuart Stryker, and Pvt. Ralph Walley the assignment of flying into combat was a new experience. Even though these U.S. privates had been trained as paratroopers, they had done all of their previous fighting as infantry troops.

Walt Leonard was struggling with the plate of a mortar that he was trying to secure inside a bundle with a rope. When Paul Hines grinned at him, Leonard scowled. But he only elicited a wider grin from Hines and the others around the private.

"Okay, I got a screwin'," Leonard huffed. "Sure, they told me to pack my bags; I was goin' back to the states. But shit, now they got me back in combat."

"Don't worry," Paul Hines said, "maybe you'll find one 'a them pretty blonde krauts and she'll let you lay her for a couple 'a chocolate bars." He leaned forward. "You did bring chocolate bars, didn't you?"

"Ah, shut up," Leonard barked.

"You wasn't as bad off as him," Pvt. Stuart Stryker nodded toward Pvt. Ralph Walley. "Three years in the Pacific and then they sent the poor bastard over here; a sergeant yet, and now he's private just like the rest of us. You shouldn't have gone AWOL, Walley."

"It was worth it," Ralph Walley grinned. "I had

116

five days with my new wife and I enjoyed every hour of it. What the hell did I have to lose? What's the difference if I'm back in this fuckin' war as a private or a sergeant?"

Then, a cry came from platoon sergeant John Queenan. "Okay you guys, IP in five minutes; check your gear for jump."

The privates stiffened. Suddenly, they ceased the small talk. In a few moments, they'd be fighting Germans again. They only hoped they'd at least hit the ground safely and get a chance to run for cover. The troopers then jerked when they heard the quick whine of a plane overhead. They knew inwardly the plane was probably a friendly fighter, one of the P-51s escorting them to the drop zone. But there was always the chance the whine had come from a German ME 109 or FW 190 fighter plane; or even worse, one of those dreaded jets they had heard so much about.

In the lead glider of the 194th Glider Infantry Regiment, the 12 men aboard the CG-4 felt like bouncing stones inside of a cement mixer. The flimsy wooden aircraft jounced, dipped, or wobbled continually as the light glider cut through the heavy air resistance behind its towing C-47. Other gliders in the formation swayed or jerked like erratic kites behind their tow planes, and some twittered erratically about the sky. Sometimes, a fellow CG-4 jerked diagonally and came dangerously close to the lead glider.

Sgt. Clint Hedrick, the 3rd Platoon leader, wondered what might happen if two gliders collided. He suspected the two aircraft would probably disintegrate like stomped on match boxes. Hedrick felt cheated. He had joined the paratroops to jump out of transport planes, but they had assigned him to a glider regiment. Like most of the other 17th Airborne veterans, the sergeant knew that many gliders often crashed with devastating impact to kill or maim most of the men aboard. Some of the flimsy craft simply fell apart or burned in midair from a single 20mm AA hit, or from a burst of .50 caliber machine gun fire. The platoon sergeant glanced at Lt. Albert Richey, the C Company executive officer, whose face appeared as sober as his own.

And indeed, Richey felt as miserable as his sergeant. The lieutenant too had joined the paratroopers to jump out of a transport, and he had also resented the assignment to a glider unit. But as a company leader, Richey could not even complain. In fact, he was expected to assure his men of the relative value and safety of glider operations—something he did not really believe. Richey stared at the GIs about him, soldiers who took this bumpy, jerky ride in glum silence. The executive officer knew their fears, and he knew that anything he told them now would not help. Richey hoped his glider would glide safely to earth before the Germans blew away the CG-4, or before the glider slammed into some obstacle that shattered the flimsy aircraft and those inside.

The 194th commander, Col. Jim Pierce, also rode in this lead glider. He looked at his watch: 0930 hours. Then he ran his tongue around his lips. In a half hour the glider would cut itself loose from its C-47 and the CG-4 would begin the descent. The colonel stared out of a window at the other gliders in his unit, CG-4s that also floundered about the sky against stiff air resistance. The 194th CO hoped that every craft landed safely for he would need every able man and every piece of equipment. He also hoped the CG-4s of the accompanying 681st Glider Artillery Regiment also landed safely because he would also need the artillery pieces, TDs, and light tanks on these gliders.

Pierce had no illusions about this mission. He did not care how many Allied guns had shelled the east bank of the Rhine, nor how many planes had saturated the enemy positions with bombs. He knew what had happened at Normandy and at Arnhem—and he knew that no amount of shelling and bombing would eliminate the enemy. Pierce also suspected that the enemy would be more determined than ever in fulfilling their Watch-on-the-Rhine. He fully expected strong resistance in the Wesel area, especially along the vital communications networks, highway, and railroads that carried men and supplies along the length of the Rhine.

The colonel looked again at his watch: 0945. Then he rose from his wooden seat and barked to his men: "IP in two minutes; two minutes. Prepare yourselves for landing in fifteen minutes."

The men did not answer. They only looked soberly at their commander.

For several more minutes the 2½ mile length

of aircraft droned on. Then, the men of the 17th Airborne heard the boom of Allied artillery that still numbed enemy positions across the Rhine; and the troopers felt the concussions of bombs from American fighter-bombers that still pasted German defenses in and around Wesel. The sounds of cannon and bombers should have brought reassurances to the U.S paratroopers, but the GIs continued to sit moodily and silently in their C-46 transports or inside their CG-4 gliders.

Soon, the airborne troops saw the changes in the terrain below. The greenery that had shone golden from the morning sunlight had now turned gray, where thousands of Allied vehicles had churned the landscape to mud before the ground troops had crossed the Rhine. The troopers also studied the endless dots of dark gray, white, black, and olive drab—countless stacks of supplies, ammo, guns, vehicles, or campsites on the west bank of the Rhine.

And soon, they saw the river itself, a snaking, murky stream that zigzagged its way from south to north. The paratroops saw nothing on the river by 1000 hours, for the LCIs and LCMs had completed their tasks of ferrying ground troops, supplies, and armored vehicles across the Rhine. The airborne soldiers guessed that ground forces by now must have surely established extensive and strong bridgeheads. It was a consolation, for the infantrymen might now be in a position for a quick link-up with the airborne troopers.

Then the troopers smelled chemical smoke, an

acid tang that stung their nostrils, and they knew they were now passing through the smoke screen that ran for miles along the east bank of the Rhine. The thousands of canisters hurled across the river to obscure the river crossing still left a lingering odor in the low sky at this late morning hour.

Soon the aircraft were east of the Rhine, but the paratroopers saw no sign of life, not a single German, vehicle, gun, or soldier. But the GIs guessed that the Germans were probably dug into hidden positions along the roads, about railroad pikes, around the Issel Canal, and inside a dozen bomb cratered towns.

In the lead C-46, Coutts pulled at his parachute straps and again rose to his feet. However, he almost fell when the plane bounced abruptly from a flak burst off the port side. The colonel squinted out of the window and saw more black puffs bursting about the huge formation of C-46s. Goddamn! After all that shelling and bombing, the krauts still managed to send up skyfuls of flak. Pierce then winced when he saw a C-46 next to his own suddenly burst into flames from a solid 88mm anti-aircraft hit. The Commando went down like a flaming meteorite to crack up and explode in the greenery below.

Coutts turned and cried to the other 23 men aboard the plane. "Okay, hitch up! Hitch up!"

The men responded quickly, staggering through the fuselage of the plane that now bounced intermittently from close anti-aircraft bursts. The 513th Regiment commander looked

at his watch and nodded before the jump sergeant slid back the wide door and air rushed into
the fuselage. The colonel hooked up and looked
once more at the men behind him before he
squinted at the landscape below. "Okay, let's go."

Then Colonel Coutts leaped out of the aircraft
before the olive drab chute blossomed a moment
later. Then came Maj. Paul Smith, several more
officers, several non-coms, and finally Pvt.
George Peters and the other few privates aboard
the plane. As the two dozen chutes drifted toward earth, Peters prayed fervently that he'd hit
the ground before the Germans picked him off in
mid-air.

In another C-54, Lt. Col. Allen Miller of the
513th's 2nd Battalion prepared to jump. He
stood at the open door and watched the hundreds
of chutes already floating to earth behind him.
Then he turned to his men. "Okay, stand up!
Check equipment and hook up!" When Miller
looked again out of the open door, he stiffened.
Flak was exploding all about the C-46 and
bouncing the plane about the sky. Miller needed
to hang on to avoid falling. The lieutenant colonel saw below and behind him the magnificent
sweep of the Rhine and then the lengths of railroad and roadway pikes ahead that skirted the Issel River and Issel Canal. He also stared at the
swarms of Allied fighters and bombers above
him.

The C-46 had dropped to below 600 feet when
the rat-a-tat of gunfire suddenly punctured the
metal frame of the plane. Nobody inside had

been hurt but the C-47 suddenly veered and dipped, apparently out of control. Then, an ashen faced crew member ran toward Miller. "They got our pilot; he's badly injured."

"What the hell are we going to do?" Miller cried.

"The co-pilot is taking over."

Seconds later, the plane straightened. "You'd better make your jump, sir," the crew member said.

Miller nodded and yelled again to his men. "Let's go!"

The 2nd Battalion commander leaped out of the plane and 23 other paratroopers quickly followed, tumbling out of the Commando like peas out of a giant pod. As they descended to earth, Lieutenant Colonel Miller stiffened with each new burst of flak or each new chatter of machine gun fire. He pursed his lips and almost coughed from the searing dryness in his throat. As Capt. Oscar Fodder came down, he kept his eyes riveted to the dozens of other chutes also floating to earth. He tried to ignore the flak bursts and the sounds of machine gun fire. In fact, he tried to count the endless expanse of colorful, falling chutes: the olive drab carrying men, the blue ones carrying guns and ammo, and the yellow ones dropping supplies, or the green with medicines and rations.

Lt. Col. Allen Miller landed in a small fenced in pig sty, just beyond his railroad tracks objective. Battalion surgeon Oscar Fodder came down right next to him. Another man had also landed in the pen, but his eyes were wide open and his head was flopped back, gushing blood. Miller turned the metal key and pressed to release his parachute, but nothing happened. Then, with Captain Fodder's help, Miller struggled to free himself from the chute. He was barely free when he heard a staccato of gun fire coming from several directions.

The lieutenant colonel and surgeon scampered toward a wooded area and here they found several dead GIs, victims of the heavy fire. Then an artillery shell exploded nearby, prompting Miller and Fodder to jump into a ditch.

Aboard E Company's plane, Capt. Harry Kenyon had been checking his equipment as the jump sergeant slid open the fuselage door of the C-46. Kenyon was about to issue fresh instructions to those aboard when a burst of flak exploded close to the plane. The men inside jerked and some even fell. Seconds later, before the E Company troopers recovered from this anti-aircraft burst, they saw smoke pouring from the fuselage from one of the wing tanks that had caught fire. Kenyon stood aghast as the radio man crewman came back to him.

"Sir, you'd better get out fast."

Kenyon nodded and then motioned anxiously to his troopers, who did not hesitate as the captain directed one after another out of the plane: Sergeant Queenan, Privates Stryker, Leonard, Hines, Walley; and the others of E Company. Then, Kenyon jumped. As the 24 troopers drifted to earth, the captain glanced upward and saw the C-46s entire left wing engulfed in flames. He hoped the crew would escape the obviously fatally damaged plane

Then Kenyon jerked from an exploding flak burst and he grimaced when he saw some of his troopers suddenly go limp from shrapnel hits or machine gun fire; or when a chute deflated from flak shrapnel that had riddled the silk. The E Company commander then watched the ground come ever closer and he prayed he would hit the earth before he suffered the same fate as some of his men.

When he alighted on earth, Captain Kenyon leaped into a bomb crater and Private Stryker tumbled right into the hole with his company commander. Other troopers of E Company also zigzagged or crawled to shelters to avoid the intense German fire that poured into the areas from inside some woods.

"Those bastards," Captain Kenyon cursed. "They said we wouldn't hit any opposition. This place is worse than Normandy. Worse!"

Pvt. Stuart Stryker did not answer.

Aboard the 194th Glider Regiment's lead CG-4, Col. Jim Pierce felt utterly drained. Within the past two minutes he had seen two gliders blown to shreds by accurate 88mm anti-aircraft guns that were spewing up flak from somewhere around the Issel Canal. Pierce expected the same fate at any moment and he turned anxiously to the glider pilot.

"Where the hell's our zone? When are we getting there?"

"In a couple of minutes, sir."

Then the glider bounced violently from a new burst of flak and the pilot turned to Pierce. "It's coming from nine and twelve o'clock, sir, but we'll make it."

The 194th commander looked at the others inside the glider, troopers who sat wide-eyed and horrified. They were scared, no question about that, for they too had seen the fellow gliders go down in cascades of fire. They too feared a similar fate before they landed. Lt. Al Richey felt his insides tighten into throbbing knots and Sgt. Clint Hedrick felt his bones ache from the tenseness that had stiffened him as rigidly as a plastic figurine. Hedrick intermittently stared agog at the bursting flak or he closed his eyes and prayed.

Then suddenly, the glider jerked as the pilot pushed the lever to cut the tow cord loose from the towing C-47. The CG-4 fell slowly to earth. During the glide, Pierce looked at his watch: 1020 hours. They were 20 minutes late. "We're going to hit! Hang on!" he warned the others.

The men saw the ground come toward them and then felt a splintering crash as the glider rammed through a fence, over a gully, and then into another fence. By the time the CG-4 came to rest, the left wing had been chopped off and the fuselage had been punctured with huge holes. The craft had also pitched itself forward.

"Now is when you pray," Sergeant Hedrick told the other enlisted men.

Luckily, the glider had floated through a cloud

of chemical smoke that had drifted far to the east and had deftly hid this particular CG-4 from German guns. The eyes of the men inside the glider watered from the acid smoke, but the tearful eyes were a much better alternative to heavy enemy fire.

When Pierce hurried out of the glider, he saw other CGs lying about crazily at all angles: listed on their sides or tipped on their noses. "Let's go, let's go," he cried to his men.

Sgt. Clinton Hedrick and the others quickly squirmed out of the half mangled glider and into a pasture. No machine gun fire was coming from anywhere and the men felt safe. Pierce gestured, but as the men moved out, little puffs of sod suddenly erupted in front of them. Then, the staccato of machinegun fire echoed again across the pasture.

"Hit the dirt!" Pierce cried.

His men did not hesitate.

Meanwhile, Capt. Fred Wittig, the C Company commander, had alighted to earth in another glider without injury, and he directed his men out of the CG-4. Then Wittig studied the scattered, distorted forms of dead GIs who had been killed by enemy fire after alighting from their gliders. The captain motioned sharply to the others of his company. "Let's get into those woods; let's get into those woods!"

Others with the captain, including Sgt. Clem Noldau, quickly followed Wittig. But as these GIs hurried toward the brake, a chatter of machine gun fire rattled across the open field, dropping several men before the American glider troops reached the safety of the trees.

Wittig scowled. "Son of a bitch! Those krauts are all over the place; all over the goddamn place!"

No one answered the C Company commander.

CHAPTER EIGHT

The 2nd Battalion of the 513th Parachute Regiment had jumped into a most perilous area, right in the midst of FJR 6 paratrooper units, a formidable enemy. Among all of the German Army Group H units, the 2nd Parachute units, such as this one under von der Heydte, were probably the toughest opponents the Allies would find east of the Rhine.

Col. Friherr von der Heydte had deployed most of his FJR 6 Regiment around Hamminkeln, with the remainder along the main railroad pike running down to Wesel. The rest of the 2nd Parachute Division, FJR 3 and FJR 5 were defending the towns of Hamminkeln and Diersfordt, the highway, and the Diersfordt Forest. The FJR 6, in its areas, had about 20 88mm guns, several self-propelled guns, and four tanks. As soon as the U.S. paratroops began floating downward from their C-47s and C-46s, the 88 guns, used as anti-aircraft, laced the air formations and descending troops with extremely accurate fire.

By the time the last 513th and 507th Regiments of the 17th U.S. Airborne Division had reached earth, the division and its IX Transport Command aircraft had suffered heavy losses. The U.S. troop carrier units had lost 44 planes shot down and destroyed, and another 322 planes damaged. The carrier command had also lost 41 airmen killed, 153 wounded, and 163 missing. The 17th Airborne had lost over 100 men killed, 200 missing, and another 50 wounded before the troopers had hit the ground.

Luckily, most occupants of these planes had already jumped before the aircraft had been shot down. But intense German fire had killed dozens of troopers as they floated to earth; or enemy AA fire had riddled their parachutes, and many U.S. soldiers fell to earth like rocks. And now, even on the ground, the Americans were still meeting rattling German machine gun, rifle, and artillery fire that came from surrounding woodlands, farm buildings or other defenses.

Many of the troopers from Maj. Paul Smith's 1st Battalion had dropped adjacent to a heavily defended village where a full battalion of Germans had opened on them with rifle and machine gun fire. GIs died abruptly or suffered wounds as they tried to free themselves from their parachute harnesses. Pvt. George Peters, the young dog-face who had ridden in the C-46 with uneasiness among 17th Airborne brass, had been among the first GIs to escape his harness. He grimaced in anger as he saw fellow soldiers dropping around him from two enemy machine gun nests.

The young soldier from Brooklyn, N.Y., charged forward in the face of the mortar attack to silence the deadly machine guns. Peters caught shrapnel in the legs from one shell. But despite heavy bleeding, he continued on. Soon, a machine gun opened directly on the 1st Battalion private. Maj. Paul Smith and the others of his battalion who had finally freed themselves of their parachutes jumped in shell holes where they occasionally lifted their heads to peer at the crawling Peters. In one of the makeshift shelters, Major Smith and his executive officer watched Peters in awe.

"Jesus Christ, they'll cut him to ribbons," the exec said.

"He's our only chance right now, our only chance," Smith answered. "We'll never get out of here with those machine guns zeroed in on us."

Peters, bleeding profusely, now caught two slugs in the legs again to erupt more spurting blood. But the Brooklynite reached a shallow draw. He then rose to his knees and tossed a grenade at the nearest machine gun nest. The explosion killed or wounded the four German occupants and silenced the gun. Almost at once, the second machine gun team fired furiously at the audacious American. Still, Peters crawled on, despite another hit, this one in the left arm. Now, almost covered with blood, he wiggled on for another 20 yards, struggled once more to his knees, and tossed another grenade. This second explosion killed three of the weapons team and prompted the fourth to scamper away.

Major Smith quickly gestured to his men who hastily followed him toward the small village. They stormed the hamlet with withering fire, including BARs and portable machine guns. Within minutes they overran the German positions, killing 40 of the enemy, wounding a dozen more, and capturing 55 prisoners.

1st Battalion had turned near disaster into the 17th Airborne's first victory of the day. But with grieved looks, Major Smith and his troops stared down at the bloody body of Pvt. George Peters.

"This son of a bitch'n war, this bitchin' war," Smith cursed.

"I can't believe a man could do that," the executive officer said.

The quiet, young soldier from Brooklyn, Pvt. George Peters, had saved his battalion at the cost of his life. He would win a posthumous Congressional Medal of Honor.

Smith left a platoon of men to occupy the village and to care for the 55 prisoners. Then he turned to his exec. "Let's find the rest of the regiment."

"Yes sir."

Meanwhile, the 2nd Battalion under Allen Miller had also jumped more than three miles from their intended drop zone, and into the jaws

Gen. Dwight Eisenhower, CinC of Allied Forces in Europe.

Field Marshal Bernard Montgomery planned and directed Operation Plunder.

Gen. William Simpson, Commander of U.S. 9th Army, launched two American infantry divisions across the Rhine in the initial attacks of Operation Plunder.

Gen. Hoyt Vandenberg, commander of the U.S. 9th Air Force, kept his airmen busy during the entire 5 day campaign.

Col. George Bickel (R) and Maj. Jim Howard (L) led the U.S. 354th Fighter Group that supported ground troops hour after hour, every day.

An American liaison man calls for air support against German defensive pocket.

Gen. Lewis Brereton directed the airborne assault phase of Plunder.

Col. Jim Pierce, commander of the 194th Glider Rgt, drew the job of clearing the Issel Canal and then helping to overrun Wesel.

Lt. Al Richey (R) and Sgt. Bill Woolfort (L), of the 194th Glider Regiment, call for help against stiff German defense.

Col. Branner Perdue, commander of the 120th U.S. Infantry Regiment, led his unit in clearing the Lippe River defenses.

Sgt. John Ramer, 120th Regiment, cleared machine gun posts to aid his company, but lost his life. He won a posthumous DSC.

Sgt. John Queenan of the 513th Regiment, led platoon in battle for five days.

Col. Jim Coutts, commander of the 513th Regiment that cleared the Wesel-Hamminkeln corridor (L). Col. Joel O'Neal, 17th Airborne Chief of Staff at (R).

Lt. Col. Allen Miller (R) of the 513th's 2nd Battalion led troops to overrun German defenses at Platte, the last defense north of Wesel. Gen. George Howell (L), U.S. Parachute Corps, congratulates Miller.

Pvt. Stuart Stryker of the 513th singlehandedly knocked out German machine gun positions to save his company. He was killed and earned a posthumous CMH.

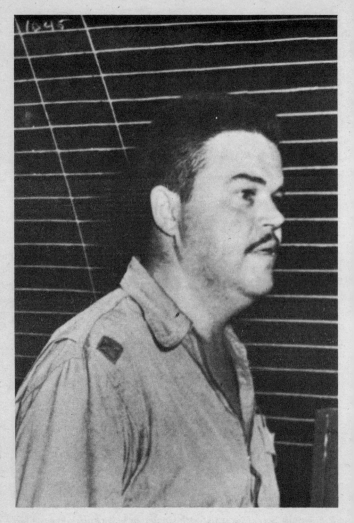

Sgt. Clem Noldau saved his platoon by knocking out a German tiger, but was killed in the action. He won a posthumous DSC.

Field Marshal Johannes Blaskowitz directed defenses of the German Army Group H to stop the Allies from crossing the Rhine in Northwest Germany.

Gen. Zengen Waldenberg commanded the 116th Panzer Greyhound Division. But his famed unit could not stem the Allied tide.

Lt. Col. Walter Harzer, commander of the Greyhound's 60th Regiment, had been very successful against Allied airborne troops in Holland during Operation Market Garden, but he could not stem the GIs of the 30th Infantry Division.

Maj. Sepp Krafft of the 60th's 2nd Battalion tried to hold the Lippe River defenses, but determined U.S. infantrymen forced him to retreat.

Gen. Walter Gericke, commander of the famed German 2nd Parachute Division, was responsible for defending the Wesel-Hamminkeln corridor, but he could not stop the U.S. 513th Regiment paratroopers.

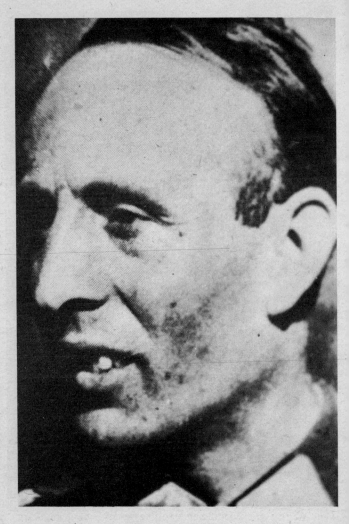

Col. Friherr von der Heydte led the 2nd's FJR 6 Regiment, a unit that had defeated heavy odds in the past, but this time he failed.

Lt. Heinz Deutsch led the company that tried to hold off the Americans outside of Platte. He was defeated and captured.

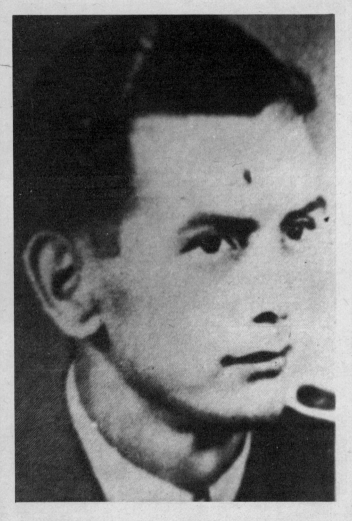

Sgt. Henrich Shafer, an Iron Cross hero in Africa, was unable to repeat his feat during Operation Plunder.

Col. Frederick Ross commanded the Wesel Volkstrum Division, but he drew an impossible task in holding Wesel against over-whelming odds. He was wounded and captured when Wesel fell.

Capt. Wilhelm Geyer of the Wesel Division's 2nd Battalion tried to hold the Issel Canal bridges, but he could not do so.

Hundreds of C-47s prepare to take off in France, carrying U.S. 17th Airborne Division troops to drop them east of the Rhine River.

American paratroopers drop by the hundreds in the Wesel-Hamminkeln corridor on the east bank of the Rhine River.

More troopers of the 513th Regiment drop across the Rhine in Operation Plunder.

GIs of the U.S. 194th Glider Regiment hurry from their gliders to seek shelter in face of heavy enemy resistance.

British glider troops of the 6th Airborne Division seek cover near Isselburg.

B-24s soar across the Rhine to drop supplies to American airborne troops.

Germans fight desperately in battered city of Wesel, but they could not stop Allied assault from three sides.

American engineers lay the first pontoon bridge across the Rhine during Operation Plunder.

Dead German troops, among 5,000 who lost their lives in trying to defend the Army Group H sector east of the Rhine.

A wounded American paratrooper awaits medical aid.

U.S. scored brilliant victory in Operation Plunder, but not all American GIs came back across the Rhine alive.

of an enemy position. The diminutive Miller gestured frantically to whatever men were with him to get under cover, and the GIs leaped into shell craters beyond a wooded area from which the enemy laced the Americans with small arms fire.

Miller had few men, for the bulk of his battalion was widely scattered. Further, the lieutenant colonel suspected that many of his men had been killed or wounded, although he had no idea of the extent of the casualties. The 2nd Battalion CO then dispatched subordinates to find as many men as possible, for in numbers there was strength. He told these underlings to bring whomever they found to the planned drop zone area where he would meet them. Then, Miller, Captain Fodder, and the others crawled swiftly through the enemy fire to reach the same drop zone area. The Americans finally escaped the Germans, and then Miller ran into Capt. Harry Kenyon who was gathering his own E Company men.

"Captain, have you seen my executive officer?"

"I'm sorry, sir," Kenyon said. "Captain Lawlor got killed while he was trying to free himself from his chute. He caught two bullets through the temple that nearly tore his head off. One of my medics found him."

"Goddamn it," Miller cursed. Then he, Fodder, and Kenyon dropped to the ground when the chatter of German machine gun fire came from a nearby patch of woods. When the barrage ended, Miller peeked up and looked at Kenyon. "We've got to get to the drop zone point. Most of our battalion might be there and so should artillery be waiting for us. We'll need guns to clear our target areas."

"Colonel," Kenyon said, "the krauts are all over the place. Maybe we ought to call in air support. We've got swarms of 9th Air Force planes upstairs."

"We can't," Miller shook his head. "Our battalion is too scattered and those fighter-bombers might hit our own guys. I've been in contact with Captain Tomosino of D Company and Lieutenant Calhoun of I Company. Tomosino's already at the drop zone and he'll wait for us. Calhoun is trying to make it the same as us."

"I never expected so much opposition," Kenyon said.

"One thing for sure," Miller said. "We can't stay here. We'll move the men southeast, Captain, to organize before we even try to take our objectives."

"Yes sir."

In a shell crater, Pvt. Paul Hines and Pvt. Stuart Stryker remained put, ducking their faces whenever they heard another rattle of machine gun fire; or they cowered deeper whenever they heard another 88mm shell scream and then explode nearby with a numbing concussion.

"Son of a bitch," Hines scowled. "They said the Air Force killed all them krauts. The bastards: the flyboys were talkin' bullshit, just like always."

"Yeh," Stryker nodded.

134

"What are we gonna do?"

"I don't know," Stryker said. He peered cautiously over the lip of the shell hole and saw only a few E Company soldiers moving about. Stryker then turned to his companion. "There's only a few guys out there. I wonder what happened to the rest?"

"They're in holes, just like us," Hines said. Then he cowered again, holding his helmet tightly, as another shell screamed over the open field and exploded somewhere off to the left. "Son of a bitch," he cursed again.

About 50 yards away, Pfc. Ralph Walley, Pfc. Walt Leonard, and S/Sgt. John Queenan also sat in a shell crater. The trio cringed whenever a new chatter of machine gun fire or whistling 88mm shells erupted from the patch of woods to the west. Walley licked his lips while his heart pounded, and Leonard wiped mud and sweat from his face. Queenan merely sat somberly, his thoughts elsewhere.

Queenan remembered vividly the heavy casualties as E Company GIs floated down from their C-46 transports. He had seen parachutists cut to ribbons from AA shrapnel before their bodies fell to earth. Others had died when flak riddled and deflated their chutes before the GIs dropped to the ground and died from the fall. Queenan had also seen troopers go limp as they caught heavy machine gun or rifle fire during the descent.

Even when the platoon sergeant hit the ground and frantically unhooked his chute, he had seen men falling around him from enemy fire; or he had seen dead men lying about the open terrain like huge green rocks.

"Sarge," Walt Leonard suddenly spoke, "what are we gonna do?" Queenan only glared at the private and Leonard continued. "Are we just gonna stay in this hole?"

Queenan shuttled his glance between Leonard and Walley, who also stared askance at the sergeant. "We'll stay here until we're ordered to do something else," the platoon leader said.

"What about the rest of the company?"

"We lost a lot of guys," Queenan said.

"How many of us made it?"

"I don't know," Queenan said. He again shuttled his glance between the two privates. "Just stay put; the captain will think of something."

Another German shell sailed over the hole and landed less than 25 yards away. The booming explosion almost deafened the trio in the crater and bounced the three GIs vigorously. They cowered even deeper into their shelter.

Beyond the almost flat terrain, where the GIs of 2nd Battalion had sheltered themselves, Col. Friherr von der Heydte stood in a bunker inside a brake and peered through the trees to study the enemy on the level plains beyond.

The Germans had received word early this morning of the expected American parachute drops somewhere on the flat plains between Hamminkeln and Wesel. The information had apparently come from captured Allied soldiers.

As soon as the Germans learned of the impending Allied airborne assault, Gen. Walter Gericke of the 2nd Parachute Division had moved swiftly. He had rightly guessed that the Americans would try to seize the towns of Hamminkeln and Diersfordt as well as key positions along the road and railroad running from Hamminkeln to Wesel. So he had deployed his three regiments as planned to meet the expected assault. He had sent two battalions of FJR 6 south of Hamminkeln, with a third battalion into the Diersfordter Forest. The FJR 3 Regiment had been implanted in the north end of the forest and FJR 5 northwest of Hamminkeln to help the German 7th Parachute Division against British attacks in the north.

Unfortunately for the Americans, most of the U.S. paratroopers had landed too far west of the assigned zone, apparently jumping too early because of the heavy German AA fire that had attacked the C-46s and C-47s. The U.S. 513th had landed for the most part just beyond the entrenched FJR 6 positions in the Diersfordter Forest. Colonel Heydte, the regimental commander, had set up dozens of machine gun posts, about ten 88mm guns, and some 15 76mm guns in the clump of forest. He had also established his FJR 6 field headquarters here and he now personally directed the heavy fire into Lieutenant Colonel Miller's 2nd Battalion ranks, most of whom were GIs from Captain Kenyon's E Company.

Thus far, Heydte's troops had done a creditable job. His forces had not only administered heavy casualties against the transport aircraft and descending American paratroopers, but he had also pinned down the Americans who had safely hit the ground. When Heydte finished peering through the trees, he walked amidst his positions.

"Have we determined how many of the enemy are out there?"

"No, Herr Colonel," a captain answered. "But, we have them immobilized. Perhaps we should attack and overrun them."

"No," Heydte said. "I will notify our other units to stop them should they attempt to move eastward or southward."

Out in the open, Lt. Col. Allen Miller waited for a momentary lull in the firing from German guns. He then scrambled out of his cratered shelter and gestured frantically. "Move out! Move to the east, the east!"

Capt. Harry Kenyon motioned to any GIs he could find. "You heard the colonel. Move it! Move it on the double!"

Lt. Dave McGuire, Sgt. John Queenan, and other leaders zigzagged swiftly to the sheltered GIs and prodded them to move. Soldiers scrambled out of their holes and ran swiftly to the east, increasing their pace when more machine gun fire or whistling shells came out of the woods. The German fire cut down several of the Americans, leaving more dead and wounded about the terrain. One GI caught two hits in the neck that nearly ripped his head off before he fell dead. Another soldier caught machine gun bullets in the chest before he died and fell.

Medics, including Capt. Oscar Fodder, defied the enemy fusillades and scampered about the open ground to drag away wounded men who had been bloodied from machine gun slugs or exploding shell shrapnel. Two of the medics caught machine gun fire themselves that killed them instantly. The battalion surgeon caught a grazing hit in the ankle from small arms fire. However, Fodder refused aid except for a bandage, and he continued to help wounded while he hobbled about the area.

Within ten minutes the Americans had escaped out of range from the enemy guns. As the GIs plodded southward, hordes of 17th Airborne stragglers converged on Lt. Col. Allen Miller's force. The newcomers had dropped in isolated fields, pasture areas, and even into a couple of abandoned German towns. By 1300 hours, Miller's battalion had swelled to several hundred men. Not only had dozens of his own troops joined the 2nd Battalion, but GIs from the regiment's other two battalions had also reached Miller's motley parade. The GIs came into the swelling mob like lost sheep herded into the fold.

As the parade plodded on, both Maj. Paul Smith of the 1st Battalion and Col. Jim Coutts, the 513th commander, had joined the group. Soon, the unwieldy mob numbered nearly 1,000 men.

"I'm sure glad to see you, Jim," Miller grinned at the colonel.

The tall, muscular Coutts nodded and then called Miller and other officers into an open field

139

conference. "We're about five miles from a major target, the town of Platte where the railroad and highway cross. I've got word that most of our 513th troops are south of us, with a battalion of 466th Regiment artillery that will give us plenty of armor, 90mm, and 105mm guns. With this help we can take that crossroad village."

Miller nodded.

"The trouble is," Coutts continued, "the area between here and Platte is loaded with German troops. We'll need to fight our way south to link up with the 466th and the other 513th troops. I'm in contact with them and they'll wait for us. I've also got a 9th Air Force liaison man with me to bring in air support."

"Yes sir," Miller said.

"I've learned from division headquarters that Colonel Roff and his 507th troopers are fighting German units around Diersfordt on the other side of the forest." He looked at Maj. Paul Smith. "Take your 1st Battalion and work your way south on the east flank."

"Yes sir."

"Allen," Coutts turned to Miller, "take your troops and move on the west flank. I'll take a few hundred men and move in the middle. If we run into trouble, we can call on flank troops for help."

"Yes sir," Miller said.

"Okay, saddle up and let's move out."

Thus, the regiment, now relatively organized into coalesced units, marched cautiously toward Platte in three columns. They had not moved far, however, before they again ran into stiff German opposition. Miller's own battalion had moved only a half mile when rifle and machine gun fire spewed from a farmhouse and two barns off the side of a secondary road. The GIs dove into ditches on the opposite side of the road while the blistering enemy fire poured from the farmhouse and two adjacent barns. Sgt. John Queenan peered over the ravine to study the enemy fire and scowled.

"Are we trapped here, Sarge?" Private Hines asked anxiously.

"It looks like," Queenan said.

"Shit, this is the second time today," Hines grumbled.

Suddenly, Captain Kenyon crawled next to Queenan, "Sergeant, do you think you can flank them and hit them with bazookas? I'll cover you."

"We'll try, sir," Queenan answered. He then turned to the men with him. "Hines, Leonard — pick up bazookas. Stryker, Walley — take BARs. Let's go."

"Goddamn bastard," Walley cursed under his breath. Why him? Why did he have to go?

The five men, however, crossed the highway without incident, while Captain Kenyon and the others of E Company sent heavy return fire into the farm buildings to keep the Germans occupied. Soon the quintet of GIs reached the side of one of the barns. Here, Queenan gestured to Hines and Leonard to ready their bazookas. The sergeant then turned from the side of the barn and fired his tommy gun. As the Germans in the barn instinctively retreated from the open window in the loft, Hines and Leonard thumped bazooka shells into the aperture. The twin b-blooms knocked out the side of the barn along with six Germans, and set the barn afire.

Queenan and his four men then hurried to the next barn where they sent more rattling BAR and thumping bazooka fire into the windows. More explosions and fires erupted, killing four more Germans and dazing a half dozen others who came out with upraised hands to surrender.

Now Queenan hit the main building from the side, while other GIs from E Company hit the farmhouse from the front. The twofold assault chopped away siding, broke windows, and started fires inside. Moments later a dozen soldiers emerged with their hands up.

"Aufgeben! Aufgeben!"

"Nice job, Sergeant," Miller told Queenan. He then turned to the others. "Okay, let's move out."

The battalion continued on for another half mile when two thumping shells exploded to the left of the American column. Once more, the GIs reacted quickly, darting off the road. When they had sheltered themselves, Miller peered through his field glasses at a large two story, elongated structure ahead of him.

"Good Christ," the lieutenant colonel said. "They might have a whole army in there. We may have to storm the building."

Once again, the chore fell to S/Sgt. John Queenan and his 1st Platoon. The non-com quickly mustered 30 men and then slithered to-ward the frame building, where four 76mm guns sent more whistling shells into the American ranks, and where a half dozen machine guns sent chattering fire in the same direction. The Germans had not seen the American platoon crawling toward them in a roundabout route, so Queenan and his men got within 20 yards of the building.

Inside the structure, German cannoneers, machine gunners, and rifle men had been concentrating on the GIs some 250 yards up the road. The Wehrmacht captain moved from window to window to warn his men. "Stay alert. The Americans may attempt a frontal attack."

"Herr Kapitan," a sergeant said, "we must drive them off soon — before they call in aircraft to attack us."

"Yah," the captain answered. The officer then urged his machine gunners and cannoneers to make a strong effort against the sheltered Americans.

The next several shells from 76mm field pieces now came much closer to the crouched 2nd Battalion GIs. And then two shells exploded directly in the midst of the troops, killing a dozen American soldiers and wounding a dozen more. Lieutenant Colonel Miller expressed shock and ordered his men to scatter to the rear.

Sergeant Queenan, meanwhile, ogled in horror at the telling artillery hits. "Goddamn it! If we don't knock out those guns, they'll slaughter our guys."

Then suddenly, chattering machine gun fire raked Queenan's own unit, killing one man outright and wounding two others. The Germans had spotted the platoon and zeroed in on the Americans. Queenan and his followers stiffened in horror. The GIs were exposed in the open, with no place to run. As Queenan licked his lips and mulled over this dilemma, Pfc. Stuart Stryker checked his carbine and grenades, sighed heavily, and then hurried forward without a word.

Queenan and the others stared in astonishment, amazed that Stryker had rushed the building alone. A burst of machine gun fire greeted the solitary GI. Two bullets caught him in the stomach, ripping open his abdomen, until his intestines became exposed. But still Stryker staggered on, firing his carbine furiously.

The private from Portland, Oregon, had drawn the enemy fire, enabling Queenan and the others to rise to their feet and storm the building. The Germans inside had been so surprised by the daring feat of this one man that the Wehrmacht soldiers had totally focused their attention on Stryker. They had not even noticed Sergeant Queenan and the other GIs storm the building.

Stryker's efforts had diverted the Germans long enough for the other dogfaces to reach the structure and send heavy bazooka and BAR fire into the long building from three sides. American shells exploded in several rooms, killing a horde of 2nd Parachute soldiers and erupting palls of choking smoke. The heavy fusillade prompted the Germans to retreat away from the frontal area, and the retirement allowed other GIs from 2nd Battalion to also charge forward in zigzagging runs to join Queenan in the assault on the building.

Soon a barrage of bazooka shells, portable 55mm artillery shells, and hand grenades poured into the building. More smoke, fire, and debris erupted, bringing screams from the wounded and dying inside.

Then came the capitulating cry from those within: "Aufgeben! Aufgeben!"

Lieutenant Colonel Miller himself aimed a tommy gun and others around him pointed BARs, while Sergeant Queenan kicked open a door. Then Private Hines and Private Walley rushed into the building and flushed out four Germans.

Moments later, Allen Miller entered the long, two story structure with a score of men while the others waited outside. Miller and his GIs soon flushed out an astounding 200 more prisoners, six 76mm field guns, several machine guns, mounds of ammunition, and boxes of grenades.

Amazingly, the 2nd Battalion GIs had also found three American airmen of the U.S. 9th Air Force who had been shot down and taken prisoner.

With the capture of this building and its horde of defenders, Miller and his men had broken the last obstacle to the objective of Platte, where they would link up with the 466th Parachute Artillery Battery and then storm the crossroad town.

Still, the GIs of 2nd Battalion looked down at the bloody, riddled body of Pfc. Stuart Stryker. Because of him, these airborne troopers had been the victors instead of the victims of this 1115 hours, 24 March, skirmish with the Germans.

Stuart S. Stryker would receive a posthumous Congressional Medal of Honor for his performance, the second 513th Regiment GI to be so honored on this first day of combat in Operation Plunder.

CHAPTER NINE

S/Sgt. Tom Martin of C Company's 1st Platoon had been inside the flimsy glider for more than three hours, and the 194th Glider Regiment non-com had become irritable and restless. He had seen the twelve men with him grow increasingly fearful as the CG-4 flopped and jerked behind the C-47 transport plane. Martin had never like this contraption that was nothing but a big crate with wings. Twice during the uneasy ride, the glider had vibrated shakily and the pilot had worked frantically to abate a tail flutter that had almost flipped over the CG-4 in mid air.

In fact, the second flutter had thrown several men violently to the floor. One man's head had jerked so abruptly that he had lost his helmet. Another man had suffered a bloody nose, becoming a casualty even before they landed.

During the long flight, the platoon non-com had watched the glider pass the Seine River, the Maas River, and the Roer plains. As they crossed toward the Rhine, Martin stared down at the shell pocked fields, the battered buildings of German villages, and the smashed city of Wesel. The sergeant also saw long, endless lines of allied vehicles that were moving east, or the patches of open farmland that were often ridged with neat patches of trees. Then, suddenly, the wind swept past the cloth covered ribs of the glider, emitting a fearful crack and snap. Martin thought the fuselage was breaking apart, but the glider held. The sergeant walked up to the pilot.

"How much longer?"

"Not long," the pilot said.

Martin returned to his skeletal bucket seat and once more stared at the men around him. Then he and the others stiffened when they heard a burst of rifle fire come from somewhere and then the pops of a burp gun, and finally the whomph of an 88mm shell that exploded off to the right in a big black puff. The men instinctively ducked or weaved, a useless maneuver inside the CG-4.

"Going down!" a cry came from the pilot.

"Brace yourselves," Martin told his men.

Then the glider jerked as the pilot cut loose the C-47. The speed slackened, the aircraft lost altitude, and the wind died down. However, as the glider neared the ground, the sound of exploding shells and rattling machine gun fire magnified to a terrifying din. The glider's right wing tilted pre-

cariously, even as the sergeant saw another glider
flit past his own. Soon the smoke of battle thick-
ened and the platoon leader felt like he was inside
of a burning building. Then as the craft neared
the ground, Martin saw other gliders parked at
crazy angles, some of them wrecked and others
burning.

Finally, the flimsy craft clipped the top of
some trees, bounced over a gully, and skidded to
a halt in a pasture. The glider had landed intact
with no one hurt.

"Let's go," Martin cried as he savagely kicked
open the door.

The GIs quickly followed their platoon leader,
spilling out of the glider. Spewing lead chopped
out little clumps of mostly green turf around the
GIs, and the men zigzagged until they reached a
barbed wire fence where two GIs quickly
snapped the wire open. Then Martin led his men
on, clawing into the earth as they crawled under
the wire. Some of the men snagged their packs on
the wire and they momentarily panicked in the
face of the continuing German fire that came
from a farmhouse 200 yards away.

Finally, Martin reached a shallow ditch and
rolled inside, splashing into nearly a foot of water in the channel bed. Still, the water felt good as
it trickled down his uniform, all the way to his
boots. The sergeant was even tempted to drink
some of the water and ease his parched throat,
but he thought better of it. He looked at the men
around him.

"Everybody okay?"

"No, Sarge," somebody answered, "our medics got hit."

"Bitch," Martin cursed. Of all the men to suffer injury, why the two medics, whom they would need so badly? One of the medics had caught a bullet through the head that had killed him instantly, and the other had caught a shot in the calf of his leg. GIs tended to the medic still alive.

Martin peered through his field glasses at the farmhouse across the field and saw shadows moving in two of the windows. How could he reach the structure to knock it out?

"Sarge," one of the GIs asked, "where's the rest of the company?"

"Scattered all over hell," Martin said.

"What are we gonna do?"

"Knock out that farmhouse if we want to move out of here in one piece."

Meanwhile, a mile to the northeast, the C Company commander, Capt. Fred Wittig, had hurried into some trees along with Sergeant Noldau. From this relatively safe position, Wittig stared into the open fields beyond and scowled. He could see two gliders burning furiously, another CG-4 caught in the trees, and two more chopped apart from heavy enemy fire. He could also see men running in terrified confusion or crawling on their bellies to avoid the heavy enemy artillery shells that erupted about the flat terrain. And soon the Germans unleashed machine gun and small arms fire, pinning down hundreds of glider troops.

Meanwhile, Sgt. Bill Woolfort and his squad

from C Company had come downward in their CG-4 toward a machine gun nest and the pilot had fired his tommy gun through the nose of the glider to silence the German position. Then the glider had ripped over some trees and scraped to a halt almost on top of another machine gun position.

"Let's go, let's go," Woolfort cried as he kicked open the door.

The others in the CG-4 hurried after the sergeant and they ran right into the startled German machine gunners. Woolfort raked the nest with spraying tommy gun fire, killing two Germans and forcing the others to surrender. The sergeant and a group of men then searched the area for more enemy positions and ran into an enemy CP. They opened fire on the building with machine guns and bazookas, drawing the other squad GIs to their side.

"There's a bunch of Germans in there," Woolfort said. "Give us a hand."

"Okay, Sarge," somebody answered.

The attack, now abetted with fire from five other men, chopped pieces of stucco from the building, shattered panes of glass, and started fires inside the structure. Then abruptly, a German major and captain came out with white flags, with about ten Wehrmacht soldiers trailing after them.

"Take them to the rear," Woolfort cocked his head.

"The rear?" a squad member huffed. "Where the hell is that?"

Woolfort grinned. "Well, stay here and guard them while we try to find the rest of the company."

"Okay, Sarge."

For nearly an hour this squad from C Company moved across open ground, through clumps of trees, and over gullies northeast of Wesel. The small group fought their way through small pockets of enemy resistance along the way.

Fortunately for the squad, a mass of vehicles and 90mm mobile field pieces had successfully landed in gliders and the artillery and armored units had split up into small groups to find and support whatever groups of glider troops they could find. One such unit had found Sergeant Woolfort and helped him to clear a pocket of Germans. With the four mobile artillery vehicles, Woolfort slogged on toward the key point near the confluence of the Issel Canal and the Issel River.

Two miles away, from a sheltered hole in some rolling terrain, Col. Jim Pierce, with Sgt. Clint Hedrick, Lt. Al Richey, and several more GIs, saw two mobile gun vehicles weaving about the fields in front of them. Pierce quickly sent out Hedrick to bring these guns to their motley unit. Meanwhile, inside the trees, almost within shouting distance of Pierce, Capt. Fred Wittig and Sgt. Clem Noldau saw a trio of TDs with 75mm guns racing over a field and he quickly directed them into the trees.

"How many more guns are coming in this direction?" Wittig asked.

"There's a couple of mobile guns up ahead," one of the gunners said. "I think they're with the colonel."

"The colonel?" the captain asked. "Good, we'll follow you and link up with him."

"Yes sir."

A mile to the southeast, S/Sgt. Tom Martin, still in his ditch with nine able men, heard the growl of two mobile artillery vehicles, and he saw them about 100 yards behind them. The sergeant quickly turned to one of his GIs. "Do you think you can get those gunners here so they can finish off that goddamn farmhouse?"

"You bet," the soldier grinned before he scampered away.

Moments later, the artillery vehicles had reached Martin's elongated ditch where the dogfaces still cowered from the machine gun and mortar fire coming from the farmhouse.

About another half mile to the northwest, Sgt. Bill Woolfort and his small group were now in the open and moving toward their objective. All along their route, 20 more men of C Company, more errant glider troops, joined the band on its way southward. Soon, Woolfort saw five TDs and a trio of mobile artillery with the 681st Glider Artillery commander himself, Lt. Col. Joe Keating, riding the lead TD. Woolfort and his men went out to meet the officer.

"Where the hell's your company?" Keating asked Woolfort.

"I don't know, sir; scattered all over."

"We'll send out small teams to round up as

many mavericks as we can. I don't give a goddamn what outfit they belong to. We're going after that Issel River bridge and I want as many
men as possible. We'll wait a half hour and then
move out."

"Yes sir," Woolfort said.

The sergeant and his men found another 100
men who joined Keating. Then the mixed group
of soldiers and mobile artillerymen moved southeast.

Some distance to the west, Captain Wittig and
his men ran into Colonel Pierce who had been
plodding southeast with his own assorted group
of GIs. The force now totalled more than 200
men, including many stragglers who had joined
Pierce's band with bazookas, 55mm portable artillery, and disassembled machine guns. Three
tank destroyers had also joined. Pierce met with
all the officers and non-coms he could find in this
motley unit.

"So far as I can tell," he referred to a map,
"we're right about here. I'd say the Issel Canal is
about a mile south of us. We'll try to reach it and
take the bridges and dams over the waterway.
We'll send the TDs in the van and the foot soldiers after them. We'll keep the heavy guns behind us for more support. Everybody
understand?"

"Yes sir," Captain Wittig said.

"Okay, move the men out."

As the mixed array of plodding GIs and armor
moved south, four more 90mm mobile artillery
crews joined them and the force continued on.

But they soon came under heavy fire from a German defense position that included two Mark V tanks and four 76mm guns. Pierce quickly scattered his troops and opened with 90mm artillery fire. The American shells struck accurately, knocking out two of the enemy guns, destroying one tank, and badly damaging a second Mark V.

"Okay, hit 'em hard!" Pierce cried.

The GIs snaked quickly forward against the clump of buildings. Wittig led one band, Sergeant Hedrick led a second, and Colonel Pierce the third. They closed on the German defenses from three directions, while the TDs and mobile guns saturated the area with 75mm and 105mm shells. The cannon projectiles flattened two of the structures, set another afire, and chopped huge chunks of earth out of the terrain. Slowly, the German fire diminished to sporadic rifle pops, while a mere infrequent mortar shell now came from the German position.

Soon the GIs sent bazooka and 55mm shells into the area, while other 194th soldiers sprayed the area with BAR and rifle fire. German soldiers tried to scamper away, but many of them caught hits and toppled to the ground, dead or wounded. Finally, Sergeant Hedrick led his unit of 20 men into the clumps of damaged and burning buildings. He overran one machine gun position and knocked out a second with hand grenades. After the sergeant and his men leaped into the smashed gun position, Hedrick peered at the structure in front of him and then turned to one of his men.

"Joe, send a couple of bazooka shells into that building. We might force them out."

"Sure."

Two subsequent explosions within the building did indeed force the Germans out. A lieutenant colonel led a parade of 50 German soldiers from the Wesel Division out of the structure, 15 of whom were injured. Moments later, Colonel Pierce and Captain Wittig rushed into one of the abandoned buildings that was the CP of the Wesel Division's 1st Battalion. The two Americans found an array of maps and charts that outlined the German defense positions on the northeast quadrant of Wesel as well as along the Issel River and Issel Canal.

"Goddamn," Pierce grinned, "we know right where they are. General Brereton will sure like this information."

"I'll send a runner back to the Rhine," Wittig said.

Pierce nodded and then squinted to the south. "Two of those enemy defense positions must be on those two bridges over the canal. We'll head for them."

"Yes sir."

Meanwhile, S/Sgt. Tom Martin had stationed the two mobile artillery pieces behind his ditch and ordered them to open fire on the farm building. The U.S. gunners responded with 90mm shells that pummelled the lonely structure in the middle of the open area. One shell blew out a small dormer on the sloping roof. A second shell disintegrated an entire front bedroom on the second floor, and a third shell chopped away a corner of the frame structure.

"You guys follow us," Martin told the artillerymen.

When the gunners nodded, the platoon leader led his men out of the ditch and moved cautiously across the open field. The artillery vehicles trailed closely in the wake of the plodding GIs, their barrels still aimed at the farmhouse. For the first several minutes only a silence and wisps of smoke came from the battered structure and Martin hoped they might have finished off the Germans inside. However, as the GIs came within 75 yards of the building, a 76mm shell exploded in their midst, followed by a rattle of machine gun fire. The GIs scattered, but not before the German fire had killed three men and wounded two more.

One GI caught heavy shrapnel from the exploding 76mm shell that ripped his torso open, throwing out his insides with a gush of blood. He convulsed twice and then lay still in death. A second U.S. soldier caught two machine gun slugs in the chest that spun him around before he collapsed to the ground. Shell fragments had ripped out the stomach of a third 194th soldier and he simply toppled over before collapsing to the ground in death.

The U.S. artillery men quickly responded and silenced both the German artillery and machine gun. Even though reduced to 14 able men, Martin continued on. The GIs crawled forward along the ground with the rumbling mobile artillery directly behind them. The Americans reached the structure with no further enemy fire and Martin rushed the building with six men.

Inside, the sergeant and his soldiers coughed from the wisps of artillery smoke that still lingered about the shattered rooms. They moved cautiously from chamber to chamber where they found bodies of contorted, bleeding German soldiers who had died at their gun posts. They found other Germans in bloody heaps next to their mangled field pieces, victims of the American 105mm fire.

"Goddamn," one of the men said, "these bastards fought to the end."

"There ain't many krauts who'll do that anymore," Martin said. "They've been quittin' as soon as they see the muzzle of an artillery piece."

"What do we do now?"

Martin took a map from his shirt pocket and studied it for a moment. He then looked out of the paneless window at the terrain in the distance. "I'd guess we're about two or three miles from the Issel Canal. Everybody we came across was headin' for that canal, so we might as well do the same thing."

Within a few minutes, the GIs climbed aboard the mobile artillery vehicles that rumbled southwest along a secondary dirt road. The fairly comfortable ride was the first respite for these men since they boarded the gliders some four hours ago. S/Sgt. Tom Martin occasionally squinted up at the sun to verify his southwest movement. He hoped he did not meet any more opposition before he reached the canal where he expected to find hordes of other 194th troops.

A mile to the south, Lt. Col. Joe Keating of the 681st Glider Artillery was also moving southwest with his three mobile guns and six TDs. He rode in one of the TDs with Sergeant Woolfort, while other GIs rode on the other vehicles that bounced over the rough terrain. Keating studied a map in his hand as he rode.

"There ought to be a road somewhere around here that leads to the canal."

"I don't remember seeing a damn thing, sir, when we came into our landing area," Woolfort said.

"Well, we'll just keep traveling southwest."

The American column moved on for about a half mile when suddenly Keating and Woolfort heard a rumble off to the right. Both men gaped for they recognized the sound of German armor. Six tanks, three light Mark IVs and three heavy Mark Vs suddenly growled out of a clearing of trees. Before the Americans saw them, the Germans unleashed machine gun fire and 76mm and 88mm shells. Huge clods of earth flew skyward from the explosions about the American vehicles. One 88 shell struck a TD squarely, blowing away the vehicle, its gunners, and six GI passengers from C Company.

"Scatter!" Colonel Keating cried.

The soldiers quickly slid off the vehicles and scampered away, deserting the area to avoid the heavy fire. However, a 76mm shell caught one clump of Americans and killed three of them in a concussioning blast that sent hot shrapnel through their bodies. Two more GIs, wounded, writhed in pain on the ground. Another shell, this one an 88, caught one of the mobile artillery vehicles and the 105mm conveyance erupted in a ball of fire, searing to death the four man crew. Luckily, GIs had abandoned the vehicle before the shell hit.

The other 681st Glider Artillery vehicles successfully weaved about the area to dodge similar hits from the ominous tanks. Finally, Colonel Keating mustered his mobile field pieces to fire back at the German Marks. One 105mm shell caught a Mark IV and the tank burst into flames. A TDs 75mm shell hit one of the Tigers and the Mark V stopped dead in its track. Two successive 75mm shells from other TDs hit the same Mark V and spun the heavy tank about, completely knocking off its treads. The three surviving tanks retreated to reassemble themselves for a duel against the Americans.

Soon both sides sent heavy shells and machine gun fire at each other. However, both the Americans and Germans had sheltered themselves quite well and neither side scored any more telling blows. In the stand-off, Colonel Keating turned to Sergeant Woolfort.

"We'll never reach that canal if we don't neutralize those tanks. And God knows, they may have a dozen more in there."

"How about air support, sir?"

"Good idea," the colonel grinned. Keating found his radio man and called the 17th Airborne liaison. "We need air support, and we need it in a hurry. We've got several enemy tanks barring our way south."

"Can you give us a coordinate?"

Keating looked at his map and then squinted about the terrain. "I'd say it's about 58.4."

"Okay, sir, we'll have some planes over to you."

The stand-off continued for about another ten minutes before Keating and his GIs heard the whine of aircraft to the east. And soon a formation of P-47s circled over the area. Then Keating got a call.

"This is A-2 support," Col. George Bickel of the 354th U.S. Fighter Group said. "Where are those enemy tanks?"

"Right in those trees across from us," Keating said.

Colonel Bickel circled again, studying the positions of the Americans, while he noted the treeline about 200 yards to the west. The 354th Fighter Group leader buzzed low over the trees and spotted not three tanks, but several heavy armored vehicles. Keating had guessed right. The Germans had more tanks there.

"Target just inside treeline," Bickel told his pilots. "We'll go in one at a time. I'll lead. Stay thirty seconds apart."

"Yes sir, Colonel," one of Bickel's airmen answered.

The American GIs watched the Thunderbolt fighter-bombers zoom over them and roar toward the tree line, where the planes unleashed clusters of 5″ rockets that exploded inside the

161

brake. The GIs then saw bursting balls of fire or erupting palls of smoke where the American pilots had scored solid hits on the German tanks. Then the dogfaces watched the P-47s arch in the sky and come back again with more whooshing 5″ rockets that pummelled the enemy under the trees. Again, balls of fire and palls of smoke erupted in the forest. Colonel Bickel called Keating.

"I think we've taken care of them. Do you need anything else?"

"How about escorting us south to the canal?"

"No can do, Colonel," Bickel answered. "We're getting more calls than a madam in a whorehouse. We've got three fighter-bomber groups out this morning and none of us has had a minute's rest. Still, if you run into more problems, call liaison. Good luck; hope you reach the canal."

After the P-47s zoomed off, Keating and Woolfort emerged cautiously from their shelter and into the open. But no enemy fire greeted them. The Americans saw only the curling smoke inside the trees and the occasional bursts of fire. Keating gestured and his surviving mobile cannon vehicles rumbled out of their shelters without incident.

"I guess those flyboys took care of them, sir," Woolfort said.

"Looks like it," Keating answered. He looked at his watch. "We're running late. I'd like to reach the canal as soon as we can. Muster the men."

"Yes sir," Sgt. Bill Woolfort said. Then the platoon sergeant barked sharply. "Okay, mount up!" Moments later, the vehicles and the GIs, most of them from C Company, again moved southwest, but warily now.

In fact, everybody from the 194th Regiment was moving south or southwest, including the 1st and 3rd Battalions. By 1130 hours, other glider infantry troops had mustered into a semblance of order before officers and sergeants looked at maps and steered their men in southerly directions from their glider landing areas north of the Issel Canal and northeast of Wesel.

Moving toward the canal were Col. Jim Pierce, and with him was Capt. Fred Wittig, Lt. Al Richey, Sgt. Clint Hedrick, and Sgt. Clem Noldau, all from C Company. Also with the colonel were several armored vehicles and some ten mobile artillery pieces. This group was now within a mile of the Issel Canal.

Meanwhile, S/Sgt. Tom Martin had come within a half mile of the canal, and he had picked up another 20 GIs along the way, most of them from other units.

Lt. Col. Joe Keating, with Sgt. Bill Woolfort and some 300 men, was also closing in on the Issel Canal.

When word of the U.S. airborne assault in the Diersfordt Corridor had reached Army Group H headquarters, Gen. Johannes Blaskowitz had ordered a deployment of troops to meet these new threats. The German field marshal had already taken measures to stop the American 79th and 30th Divisions that had crossed the Rhine several hours earlier and he now needed to protect both the corridor and the Issel Canal waterway.

Blaskowitz had ordered the parachute divisions to protect the corridor between Isselburg and Wesel, which Gen. Walter Gericke of the 2nd Parachute Division had done quite nicely. His FJR 6 Regiment under Colonel Heydte had acted especially well in mauling the U.S. transport planes and the descending American paratroopers. Blaskowitz had also called on the Wesel Volkstrum Division to guard the canal and Col. Frederick Ross had sent a full battalion to bolster the Issel Canal defenses. Meanwhile, the German field marshal had called on the 15th Panzer Division in Elms to alert its units so they could offer reinforcements wherever necessary.

Capt. Walter Geyer of the Wesel Division's 2nd Battalion had alerted his men who were holding the dams and bridges over the Issel Canal, while a regiment from the 15th Panzer Division, far to the northeast, moved swiftly southward to take up positions along the Issel River. By 1130 hours, Captain Geyer's 600 troops, including Lt. Heinz Becker, were well entrenched on the bridges and dams about the Issel Canal.

Captain Geyer had with him, besides his full battalion and the cadre of paratroopers from the 7th Parachute Division, 20 88mm and 76mm self-propelled artillery pieces, 16 machine gun teams, and seven Mark V tanks that he had borrowed from the 116th Panzer Division. Now Geyer stood on one of the bridges over the canal with Lieutenant Becker, and the captain peered to the north through his field glasses.

"Do you see anything, Herr Geyer?"

"No, Lieutenant," the 2nd Battalion commander said. "But, there is no doubt that American glider troops are on their way from their landing areas to the north. We have word that many units have attacked these enemy forces as they came south."

"Can we hold them?"

"It is my understanding that the American glider troops included about a regiment of troops. However, I was told that hordes of them were destroyed, so the Americans cannot number more than five hundred able men. I believe we can repel them with our battalion and the company of troops who are on the way as our reinforcements."

"What of their Air Force?" Lieutenant Becker squinted up at the sky.

"That could be a problem," Geyer admitted. "But we can expect some Luftwaffe help from our jet gruppens. Come, we will make one more tour of our defenses to make certain we are prepared."

"Yes, Herr Geyer," Lieutenant Becker answered.

CHAPTER TEN

The death of Pvt. Stuart Stryker had depressed the GIs of E Company because his actions had obviously saved a score of these paratroopers. Still, the private's death could not hold up the war. Soon enough, Lt. Col. Allen Miller cleared the clump of farmhouses. He then sent the German prisoners and the liberated airmen to the regimental field headquarters, now established between Hamminkeln and Wesel. Then he moved his men on.

Lieutenant Colonel Miller, like other battalion commanders of the 513th Airborne Regiment, suffered from a lack of supplies because of the heavy opposition in the 513th's drop sector. The Americans had only secured about half of the provisions dropped with the airborne troops. In fact, many of the bundles had fallen into enemy hands. Luckily, however, many of the wayward GIs who had joined Miller had carried supply bundles with them. Thus as he neared his objective, the railroad-highway junction at the south end of the Diersfordter Forest, Miller had garnered considerable provisions.

But the 2nd Battalion commander expected strong resistance at this target area, the crossroad town of Platte. In fact, Col. Friherr von der Heydte had rushed many of his men south from the forest to bolster other FJR 6 troops in Platte. The colonel had guessed rightly that the Americans were heading for this crossroad town and, when he had done all he could at the American drop zone, he had quickly ordered whomever he could spare to rush south and join the defenders at Platte.

Shortly after noon, 24 March, on a signal bridge over the railroad pike just north of Platte, Lt. Heinz Deutsch squinted to the north. Next to the A Company commander stood Sgt. Heinrich Shafer. The two men had only slept a few hours last night and they had only eaten a simple meal of sauerkraut and black bread this morning in the battalion mess hall inside Platte. After rechecking their defenses, they had resumed their vigil on the signal bridge. The Germans in and about Platte would attack the southbound Americans as soon as they came into view, either down the Hamminkeln Highway or over the Isselburg-Diersfordt Railway pike. Deutsch's A Company would probably be the first unit among the Platte defenders to engage the enemy.

"How soon do you think the Americans will get here?" Sergeant Shafer asked.

"We were told they jumped a couple of hours ago, both east and west of the Diersfordter Forest," Deutsch said, "just south of Hamminkeln. We know that elements of these enemy airborne troops are coming south because many of our troops have resisted them along the way, especially at Diersfordt. I do not believe the Americans can possibly reach here before mid-afternoon. And if our resistance to the north was successful, perhaps they will not get here at all."

Sergeant Shafer nodded, but he doubted that German units to the north were strong enough to stop the U.S. troops. "Lieutenant, do we have enough guns and armor in the Platte area to stop them?"

"We have six Mark IVs and twenty-two field pieces, including a dozen 88mm self-propelled cannon. Colonel Heydte has also established twenty machine gun positions inside Platte, with at least as many panzerfaust teams (anti-tank weapons similar to the American bazooka). I believe we have the means to stop our enemy, especially since the Americans no doubt lost many troops during their jump east of the Rhine River."

"Let us hope so," Shafer said.

Then Deutsch got a call from battalion head-quarters in Platte. "Lieutenant, you must be alert. We are told that a column of Americans are

169

a mile north of you. We cannot be sure, but we believe they have armored vehicles and artillery with them."

"We will be ready for them and repel them as soon as they come into range."

"Good," the battalion staff officer said.

Deutsch alerted his two machine gun teams on the signal bridge and the two at the foot of the bridge. The A Company officer then called for several panzerfaust men, one for each of his machine gun teams. He wanted his troops as heavily armed as possible to hurl back the first American strike.

Lt. Col. Allen Miller, meanwhile, had indeed brought his column to within a mile of Platte, and he now peered to the south through his field glasses. He saw faintly the German soldiers on the signal bridge and he saw the hazy outlines of armor and artillery pieces in the village beyond. He turned to Harry Kenyon, the E Company commander.

"Captain, we'll take a ten minute break here and then send the TDs ahead. I've got a feeling we're going to need plenty of grit to take that town. It looks like the area is heavily defended."

"Yes sir."

After a rest, the Americans moved on, with E Company in the lead.

The GIs had not marched more than 500 yards when they ran into a two story structure where a Red Cross flag fluttered from the roof. As Kenyon cautiously approached the building, he turned to John Queenan. "Sergeant, that looks like a hospital of some kind, but we'll have to attack anyway, unless they're willing to surrender. Take a half dozen men, get close, and open with small arms fire, just enough to make them give up."

"Yes sir."

Queenan then cocked his head to a group of men, including Private Hines, Private Walley, and Private Leonard. When the men came within 50 yards of the building, the sergeant gestured to his men, who moved off the shoulders on both sides of the road. Then on Queenan's signal, the GIs sent rifle fire into the building, chopping away some of the stucco from the walls or smashing window panes. A moment later, a white flag fluttered from two of the windows.

"I guess they'll give up," Queenan said. "Let's go."

The GIs rose to their feet and moved cautiously forward. "Come out of there," Queenan cried. "Kommen! Kommen aus!"

However, the Germans responded with a storm of small arms fire from three windows, wounding one of Queenan's men. The others quickly hit the dirt.

"The sons 'a bitches!" Queenan cried. He looked at Walley who carried a bazooka. "Let 'em have a few of those shells."

"A pleasure," Walley scowled.

A moment later, the private whooshed three bazooka shells, one through each of the three windows, erupting a trio of explosions that shattered the area and wrecked parts of the building walls. Flames and smoke then whooshed out of the structure and Queenan rose to his feet to shout again.

"Kommen aus! Kommen aus!"

"Aufgeben," a voice responded from within the smoking building.

"If you're giving up, then get your asses out here," Queenan cried again.

This time, the Germans did not fire. They poked a white flag out of the front doorway and an officer wearing a Red Cross band came out first. "Aufgeben," he said softly. Queenan gestured to his men who hurried forward to meet the obvious German doctor, as several other Germans came out of the building.

"Do you speak English?" Queenan asked sharply.

"Yah," the doctor nodded.

"Are there any more of you inside?"

"Just the wounded and some dead who were killed by your shelling."

"That was your fault," the American sergeant gestured icily. "Who the hell was in there shooting at us after you put out a white flag?"

"I do not know," the German doctor answered.

Queenan turned to Private Walley. "Ralph, go back and tell the captain the place is secured."

"Okay, Sarge."

The GIs then entered the building to make certain that no more snipers were hiding inside. But, as the German physician had told them, only five dead Germans and another 20 wounded, lying in

172

makeshift hospital beds with torn pieces of cloth as bandages, greeted the Americans. The Germans were obviously low on medicine, bandages, and other supplies. Their surrender at this improvised field hospital proved to be a boon for them, because within an hour American medical teams had treated them with good medication and bandages.

The U.S. combat troops continued southward toward Platte, but quickly ran into more German resistance. Only a few hundred yards below the hospital, a sudden trio of 88mm shells exploded from somewhere off the side of the road. Two of the shells fell short, but one near miss killed two men and wounded three others.

"Take cover," Miller cried.

The GIs once more scampered off the road and dove into ditches as more 88mm shells whizzed into the area. The accompanying TDs also bounced off the road, but they turned and fired their 75mm guns. One shell exploded next to a German position, killing the gun crew and destroying the weapon. Other TD shells struck other German positions and the enemy fire slackened. Captain Kenyon took about 30 men and hurried forward through a patch of trees until he was only 25 yards from an enemy position without detection. Kenyon saw the German gunners near the 88mm barrels, and they were momentarily off balance from the heavy TD fire, with little chance to reload their weapons.

Kenyon turned to Sergeant Queenan. "Take twelve men and move behind them. I'll wait exactly two minutes and then we'll hit them from two sides. That may convince them to give up."

"Yes sir," Queenan said.

As Kenyon's group split, the E Company commander radioed Lieutenant Colonel Miller to hold up on TD fire. As soon as the 75mm fire ceased, the Germans composed themselves to begin reloading their weapons. Kenyon looked anxiously at his watch. He could not yet attack, even though the enemy shelling resumed. One shell blew up another TD and damaged a second, while keeping Miller and the rest of the 2nd Battalion paratroopers quite pinned.

The Germans had seemingly regained the initiative, but the Americans won a respite when a flight of P-47s suddenly droned over the area and the Germans jumped into shelters to avoid an expected air attack. Kenyon shuddered. Surely, Miller had not called for air support when the E Company commander and his 40 men were almost on top of the German gunners? If the American Thunderbolts attacked with rockets and machine gun fire, they would hit Kenyon and his men. But the P-47s were not after these German guns. The Thunderbolts simply zoomed beyond the area. Kenyon sighed in relief.

Luckily, the German hesitation enabled Kenyon to act successfully. The two minutes had elapsed and as the Germans came out of their holes and back toward their cannon, the captain opened with tommy gun, BAR, and bazooka fire. The surprised Germans suffered four men killed and several injured. They hurried to the side of their weapons for shelter, but then caught rattling fire from the rear as Sergent Queenan and his party opened on the Wehrmacht artillerymen. This second fusillade left more Germans dead. One of their number then uttered the now increasingly familiar cry:

"Aufgeben! Aufgeben!"

"Kommen aus!" Sergeant Queenan shouted.

A dozen Germans then emerged with upraised hands from the patch of woods that had sheltered their artillery pieces. Captain Kenyon sent them to the rear under four guards, while Queenan entered the area to examine the big guns.

By 1400 hours, the U.S. 2nd Battalion was again on the move. They met no more resistance and within a half mile of Platte, Lieutenant Colonel Miller once more peered through his field glasses to verify his earlier suspicions. The signal bridge and the town itself were indeed quite heavily defended.

"Colonel, do you think they'll fight hard to hold that town?" Kenyon asked.

Miller nodded. "If they lose that junction, they won't be able to get a damn thing into Wesel from the north either by rail or by road."

"Are we going to attack?"

"Yes," Miller said, "and our first task is to take that signal bridge. That position is serving the Germans as a good outer defense as well as an observation post. Captain, take about forty men and approach the bridge through the ravine that skirts the rail bed. Move low and easy so you re-

175

main undetected as long as possible. We'll move down the road to draw their attention. We'll have TDs to shelter us; that armor won't be hurt by small arms fire."

"Yes sir," Kenyon answered.

About 300 yards from the signal bridge, a pair of American TDs unleashed 75mm shells. The explosions fell short of the bridge, but certainly drew the attention of Lieutenant Deutsch and Sergeant Shafer. The two men immediately directed machine guns on the Americans in the distance and chattering fire spewed from the German weapons. Lieutenant Deutsch then peered at the Americans through field glasses.

"They are too far away," he frowned. He called the battalion commander inside Platte. "The enemy is about three hundred fifty meters to the north on the highway, and they have mobile artillery with them."

"So they have come," the battalion commander answered with quiet resignation.

"Yes, Herr Oberst," Deutsch answered. "I believe we should fire artillery to drive them off."

"We are short of shells," the lieutenant colonel said, "but we will do what we can. I will fire one shell at a time until you assure us we are striking the enemy's exact position."

"Yes, Colonel," Deutsch said again. Then the lieutenant peered once more through field glasses and watched the first artillery shells come out of Platte. The projectiles exploded in front of the Americans and Deutsch called battalion headquarters again. "You are fifty meters short.

Please adjust range."

"Yes, Lieutenant."

Soon, another shell whistled northward. This one, although on the correct lateral, fell too far to the right and missed the Americans by a wide margin. Unfortunately, Lieutenant Deutsch had been so intent on directing artillery that he had not noticed Kenyon and his soldiers coming toward the signal bridge along the gulley off the railroad bed. Further, the German soldiers on and about the bridge, including Sergeant Shafer, had also been staring at the Americans in the distance, and they too had ignored anything else. By the time Deutsch called again to adjust range, Kenyon had come within an astonishing 20 yards of the bridge.

"Okay, open up," the American captain shouted.

A rattle of BAR, rifle and machine gun fire poured onto the signal bridge. The bullets pinged off the metal trusses and stairways, or chopped away pieces of rust on the iron surface. Some bullets caught a few of the machine gunners, killing or wounding them. Deutsch looked down in horror at the American assault party and he turned quickly to the other machine gunners.

"Open fire!"

But a pair of bazooka shells caught the second four man machine gun team on the bridge, snuffing out their lives in a shattering explosion. Continued bazooka fire and automatic fire pinned down the machine gunners at the foot of the bridge, enabling Kenyon to rush the base of the span on the left, while Queenan scampered across the tracks and reached the right side of the bridge. Kenyon's unit quickly overran a nest, forcing the Wehrmacht soldiers to surrender. Meanwhile, Queenan and his men scampered up the stairway on the east side of the span, their guns blazing, and forcing the few survivors in the area to retreat toward the west end of the signal bridge.

Then Captain Kenyon and the other American soldiers rushed up the other stairway, guns blazing. Soon, the captain stood at the opposite end of the catwalk with his tommy gun, while Queenan stood on the east end with an aimed BAR. Deutsch, Shafer and three others on the catwalk raised their hands in surrender. They could do nothing else.

Young Sgt. Heinrich Shafer would be shipped to the U.S. as a POW at Camp Harne, Texas, where in August of 1945, the camp commander would deliver to the German paratrooper a Knight's Cross that the German sergeant had earned a long time ago, while successfully defending a hill in the Faid Pass in Tunisia in 1943. After the war, Shafer would return to his native village on the Neckar River to resume his pre-war civilian job as a barge skipper on the Neckar Canal.

Lt. Heinz Deutsch, a man who had fought valiantly at St. Lo during the Normandy invasion, who had killed British paratroopers at Nijmegen during Operation Market Garden, and who had led successful attacks against British units along the Maas River, was now an American prisoner. Deutsch would escape his captors on the way back to the Rhine river bank, but he would fall into the hands of the British several weeks later at Oldenburg during the surrender of the German 1st Parachute Army.

Meanwhile, on this signal bridge, Deutsch refused to tell the Americans anything about the defenses inside Platte, and he had urged those with him to do the same.

Lt. Col. Allen Miller made no threats against Deutsch or the others for their refusal to talk. The American commander abided by the rules of the Geneva Convention. Miller simply sent his prisoners to the rear. Then the U.S. 2nd Battalion commander looked at the town and then at his watch: 1500 hours. Ironically, Lieutenant Deutsch had guessed correctly—the Americans would probably approach Platte at mid afternoon.

Miller was not about to make a frontal attack against the heavily defended town. He called for U.S. air support, asking that American planes reconnoiter the German defenses and then attack such defenses to open the way for his battalion. Once again, Col. George Bickel and the pilots of the 354th Fighter Group drew the task. Bickel first sent two of his P-47s over the village to locate the German guns and tanks. Then, Bickel mustered his Thunderbolts to hit the town.

"We'll strike at low level in pairs," the colonel told his fliers.

The P-47 pilots then whizzed over Platte with

rattling machine gun wing fire and zooming rockets. The American attack destroyed five big guns and two tanks, while setting several buildings afire, including the German battalion CP. While the airmen kept the defenders running frantically to seek cover, Miller rushed his men forward and charged into Platte.

The first resistance inside the village came from a machine gun post and Capt. Harry Kenyon turned to Sergeant Queenan. "Cover me. I'll knock it out."

After the sergeant nodded, Kenyon crawled swiftly and quietly forward while his men sent BAR and rifle fire at the German gunners who intermittently sheltered themselves from the American bullets and unleashed machine gun fire of their own. The Germans did not even see Kenyon come up to their nest, and the American captain rose suddenly to his feet to spray the four German defenders with submachine gun fire. The Germans spun around and then toppled dead in pools of their own spurting blood.

Unfortunately, Germans in a second machine gun nest had seen Kenyon attack and they quickly swerved their barrel to unleash a stream of fire. Several slugs ripped into Kenyon. But even as he fell, he hurled a grenade. The explosion fell short, but peripheral shrapnel slightly wounded two of the Germans and prompted the Wehrmacht soldiers to abandon their gun positions and retreat.

Others from E Company rushed forward and occupied the nest, but they looked down in anguish at their slain, bloodied commander who had probably saved many of his GIs from death or disability.

Now the 2nd Battalion troops pressed through the village, overrunning gun positions, flushing German soldiers from shelters, and knocking out enemy weapons. A platoon of GIs got pinned by small arms fire from a battered building and Sgt. John Queenan wiggled toward the house with two men while the rest of the platoon exchanged fire with the German defenders inside. Queenan soon reached the base of the house and ordered his two men under cover. Then Queenan yanked the pin of a grenade and tossed the explosive through the window. The burst bounced the 1st Platoon sergeant off the ground, but also erupted a ball of smoke within the building. Queenan then rose to his feet and tossed a second grenade through the window, and the explosion blew out a wall. The firing inside the house stopped abruptly.

"Kommen aus!" Queenan cried.

Four Germans responded and emerged with hands raised behind their necks.

For another hour, Lt. Col. Allen Miller and his troops worked their way through Platte, knocking out more enemy positions and taking more prisoners. By 1800 hours, just before dark, the Americans had secured Platte and forced the remnants of the German battalion to run off. The vital crossroad town was now in American hands.

Meanwhile, Col. Jim Coutts had successfully

led the paratroopers of the 513th's 3rd Battalion along the railroad pike abutting the Diersfordt Forest and at about the same 1800 hours, Coutts had emerged at the south end of the forest. He and his troops had taken 200 prisoners along the way.

To the east, Maj. Paul Smith and his 1st Battalion from the 513th Regiment had cleared their sector to occupy the vital areas along the Isselburg-Diersfordt railroad pike. They too had taken large numbers of prisoners. By 1900 hours, Coutts' three battalions had rejoined in Platte and the colonel was quite satisfied with his regiment's efforts on this first day across the Rhine.

The 513th Regiment had totally sealed off Wesel from the north to cut off any chance of reinforcements coming into the battered Rhine River city from Hamminkeln or Isselburg. Also since they jumped this morning, the 513th GIs had taken over 1200 prisoners, knocked out 50 field pieces, and destroyed 20 tanks. Finally, they had overrun five villages, including the strategic crossroad village of Platte.

Unfortunately, the 513th Parachute Regiment and attached tank and artillery units had suffered considerable losses: 159 men killed, 522 wounded, and 840 more American paratroops missing. However, 600 of the missing were simply lost and they eventually joined their units.

"Okay, we'll camp in Platte until morning," Col. Jim Coutts told his battalion commander. "I'll check with 17th Airborne headquarters to find out where they want us next."

"How about the 507th, Jim?" Allen Miller asked.

"They've taken Diersfordt and they're moving southeast directly toward Wesel. I expect them to swing east to pursue retreating German troops. My guess is that we'll be doing the same thing."

Allen nodded.

"Bed the men down for the night," Coutts said, "but make sure we keep plenty of posted sentinels."

The weary men of the 513th would need a good night's rest, for the Germans were not yet finished. Tomorrow would be another busy and harrowing day.

CHAPTER ELEVEN

Three plodding groups of GIs from the 194th Glider Regiment, soldiers with Colonel Pierce, Lieutenant Colonel Keating, and Sergeant Martin, respectively, were all marching toward the Issel Canal. They numbered more than a battalion of men with most of them from 1st Battalion. The other two 194th battalions were moving north toward the Issel River defenses.

The American glider troops had suffered substantial losses, but they still numbered more than 1,200 able troops among the three battalions, with about another 1,000 troops from the 681st Mobile Artillery. These units had about 100 TDs, mobile guns, and self-propelled guns and company size 681st units had linked up with many of the plodding 194th units, so that most of the glider troop groups had TDs and mobile artillery with them.

Further, the gliders had successfully landed more than 300 vehicles of all types, from jeeps to 6x6 trucks, along with 50 or 60 light Sherman tanks. Thus Col. Jim Pierce had plenty of help in the vicinity to assault the Issel Canal and Issel River defenses.

By noon, 24 March, Pierce had set up portable radios to maintain contact with his 2nd and 3rd Battalion commanders. He learned that both units had over 600 able men along with a large array of tanks, TDs, and mobile guns. The 2nd Battalion was about two miles northeast of the colonel's own motley unit and the 3rd Battalion was less than three miles away.

"I want at least a company of men and as many tanks as you can spare," Pierce told the 2nd Battalion commander. "We've only got about a company of men with us and we need as big a force as possible to hit the canal. You can take the rest of your battalion and join 3rd Battalion to hit the Issel River defenses."

"Yes sir."

Pierce also made contact with the commanders of E and F Companies from this 1st Battalion and he learned that these two companies had about 300 able men between them, along with seven Sherman tanks. He ordered them to join him at once for the march on the canal.

"We'll move easy," Pierce told Captain Wittig, "and let them catch up."

By 1300 hours, the men of E and F Company,

along with the company from the 2nd Battalion had joined Pierce. So too did 14 TDs, 11 Sherman tanks, and 20 pieces of mobile 105mm artillery reach him. Thus the colonel's ranks had swollen from 100 men to more than 1,000 while he also had considerable armor and artillery.

Pierce's principal problem was a lack of ammunition, for the 681st Glider Artillery had lost 60% of its ammunition during the glider landings. Pierce called the 17th Airborne headquarters and spoke to the chief of staff.

"We've mustered quite a few men, a good number of tanks and plenty of artillery, but we lack ammunition. We need 75, 90, and 105 shells in a hurry."

"Colonel, more than two hundred Liberators are out in force to make drops. At least fifty of them are carrying ammo, everything from carbine rounds to 105mm shells. Give me your position and I'll have an air drop in your area."

"We're about two miles northwest of the canal target and maybe four miles northeast of Wesel." Pierce checked his map. "Our coordinate is about 60.1."

"Okay. Stay put. You should have supplies within a half hour."

"Good," Pierce answered.

True enough. Shortly after the 17th Airborne troops had jumped in parachutes or landed in gliders across the Rhine, the 2nd Air Division of the U.S. 9th Air Force had begun its task of dropping supplies by air to any units who needed them. The 9th had coordinated planning with the

21st Army Group staff and had assigned 24 Liberator squadrons, about 250 aircraft, to begin their supply drops at 1300 hours. Such drops would be made in tightly packed, 145 pound bundles from an altitude of 200 or 300 feet.

Before this 24 March day ended, the B-24s would drop 682 bundles of supplies to 17th Airborne units, including 80,000 pounds of ammo, 2,000 artillery shells, 49,000 pounds of food and medicine, and 45,000 pounds of other provisions. The Liberator groups would lose three heavy bombers to Luftwaffe fighter planes, and 15 more to German AA guns. But an astonishing 86% of the drop loads would fall successfully and undamaged into the hands of American troops.

At 1315 hours, 20 Liberators from the 389th Bomb Group soared over Colonel Pierce's position north of the Issel Canal and dropped 156 bundles. Among the provisions were 500 artillery and tank shells, as well as a 100 crates of .50 caliber machine belts, boxes of rifle rounds, bazooka shells, and 55mm shells for the portable artillery. The drop also included countless cartons of medical supplies, cigarettes, and hordes of K rations. The 194th Glider troops quickly recovered the bulk of these provisions. Thus the GIs had ample food and ammo for the assault on the canal.

By 1400 hours, Col. Jim Pierce called together his commanders and studied his maps with them.

"There are two dams here, and two bridges here," he pointed. "If we take them and set up strong positions, the Germans can't send anything down the canal into Wesel." He looked at Fred Wittig. "Captain, take your company and E Company to hit the bridges just outside of Wesel. I'll take the rest of this force and hit the dams above the bridges."

"Yes sir," Captain Wittig said.

Moments later, Wittig led over 500 men from C, E, and F Companies, six tanks, and eleven 105mm mobile artillery pieces toward the Issel Canal bridges. Wittig's unit moved for about a half hour and they had come within a mile of the canal when 88mm artillery shells from somewhere to the south struck nearby with numbing explosions. The captain quickly directed his infantry, tank, and artillery units to cover. Then Wittig called on Clem Noldau.

"Sergeant, take a small team and reconnoiter. Try to get an idea where those guns are, and we'll open with 105 artillery."

"Yes sir," Noldau said.

The sergeant and six men crawled steadily forward and soon spotted two 88mm gun positions. While several gunners were busy at their pair of artillery pieces, ten more Germans with rifles loitered nearby as sentinels. Noldau decided to silence the guns himself instead of reporting the enemy positions and hoping that U.S. artillery could do the job. The sergeant fingered the grenades around his waist and then whispered to his companions.

"Cover me; I'll get the bastards."

"For Christ sake, Sarge," one of the men answered in a harsh whisper, "there's too many of 'em."

"Cover me," Noldau said sharply.

A moment later, Noldau reached the gun positions and he tossed two grenades. One of them exploded directly on the breech of one gun and killed all three German artillerymen. The second exploded to the left of the other gun and maimed these other gunners. However, before Noldau could toss more grenades, the German sentinels opened fire and shattered Noldau's chest and stomach. The sergeant fell, firing his carbine as he died.

Yet Noldau's efforts had diverted the Germans' attention long enough for the other GIs to rush forward with blazing BAR and rifle fire. Several more Germans fell, dead or wounded, and the others quickly surrendered.

"Aufgeben! Aufgeben!"

Noldau's team rounded up the six surviving Germans, including their wounded, and they prodded the dead Wehrmacht soldiers to make certain they had been slain. Then the GIs grimaced, when they looked down at their bloodied sergeant.

"Son of a bitch," one of the GIs cursed.

A second GI stared down at the sergeant and also cursed. "This fuckin' war! This no good, fuckin' war!"

Sgt. Clem Noldau's efforts had eliminated the last obstacle on the road to the Issel Canal, but he had lost his life. The quiet man from Wausau, Wisconsin, who had already won a Silver Star, would now win a posthumous DSC.

Now Capt. Fred Wittig continued on with his troops. Soon, he saw clearly the two bridges over the Issel Canal. The C Company commander also saw six artillery pieces and four Mark IV medium tanks. He decided to open with artillery, while he brought up his tanks and sheltered his soldiers behind them. When he was ready, Wittig gave the order.

"Fire!"

A thundering barrage of 105mm shells barked from his eleven artillery guns and exploded in numbing concussions in and about the canal. Capt. Wilhelm Geyer, the German commander of the Wesel Division's 2nd Battalion, had been expecting the attack. However, he was surprised that the shelling had come so soon. He cowered in his bridge position with Lt. Heinz Becker as the American shells erupted around him. One shell knocked out a Mark IV, while other shells knocked out two guns, and more shells blew away some of the German machine gun positions. Other Wehrmacht soldiers of 2nd Battalion scurried about in panic to avoid death or injury from the heavy artillery assault. Also, amidst the heavy attack, Captain Geyer could not clearly see the U.S. forces. Still, he ordered a counter barrage.

"Fire! Fire!"

76mm shells from the medium tanks and 88mm shells from the self-propelled guns opened into the area to the north. However, because of poor observation, the shells fell short and did little damage to Captain Wittig's troops. The C Company commander studied the rattled and disorganized German defenses and he decided to move quickly with his men and armor.

"I want artillery going until I tell you to stop. The rest of us—let's go."

The six Sherman tanks rumbled forward, their barrels thumping 75mm shells ahead of them, and their machine guns spitting deadly fire from their forward apertures. Before the Germans saw clearly the advancing Americans through the heavy artillery smoke, the U.S. forces came within point blank range of the two bridges. Wittig then called off the artillery barrage, while the American M-4 medium tanks fired their guns. The light Shermans had never been a match for the German Mark tanks, but at this near point blank range, and with the Germans in disorder, the M-4s proved quite effective.

While the tanks pummelled the German defenses, the GIs zigzagged forward, firing rifles, BARs, bazookas, and portable 55mm artillery. Sgt. Clint Hedrick led a platoon that swept away defenders at one of the canal bridges and he then stormed onto the bridge and rushed quickly forward. German troops at the south end responded with sporadic fire against the heavy, determined American charge. Hedrick drove the Germans off the span and led his GIs down the other side. The C Company sergeant then cornered a large number of Germans in an underground bunker.

"Kommen aus!" Hedrick cried.

The Germans answered with small arms fire

that scattered the GIs.

"The bastards," Hedrick cursed. He then gestured to three men who hurried forward and lobbed grenades to the foot of the bunker. The staccato of blasts loosened mounds of dust that cascaded in front of the locked entrance of the bunker.

"You bastards," Hedrick cursed again, "come out of there or we'll bury you inside. Kommen aus!"

The exploding grenades apparently convinced the Germans to surrender. If the Americans used enough explosives, especially artillery shells, enough dirt would fall to indeed entomb those inside the bunker. The steel door opened, a white flag fluttered, and then 20 Wehrmacht soldiers marched out with hands up.

"Any more of you inside?" Hedrick gestured toward the bunker. "Innen?"

"Nein," a German soldier answered.

Meanwhile, fighting continued near the other bridge over the canal. The defending Germans saw their ranks decimated and disorganized by the artillery barrage and the GI assault. The Volkstrum soldiers slowly collapsed as the Americans relentlessly cleared out the machine gun nests, rifle team trenches, and artillery positions. The determined glider troops also fired bazookas at the German tanks, wrecking treads, erupting fire and smoke, or knocking off turrets. More of Geyer's 2nd Battalion retreated in panic or gave up.

Atop the bridge itself, however, Captain Geyer

and Lieutenant Becker made a valiant stand. They fired back with burp guns and two machine guns toward the GIs under Wittig trying to cross the bridge.

"The sons 'a bitches!" Captain Wittig cursed. "I'd like to blow them to hell, but I want to take this bridge intact." He turned to one of his subordinates. "Just throw small stuff at them: 55mm and bazooka shells."

"Yes sir."

A moment later, two bazookas and a pair of 55mm projectiles whooshed across the bridge. Two of the missiles hit and exploded directly into one of the machine gun positions. Another shell near missed the second gun position, wounding two of the Germans and forcing the others to abandon the gun. Now with the machine gun defenses gone, Geyer and Becker had little with which to defend.

"Move it, move it," Captain Wittig cried, gesturing to his GIs.

As the American soldiers swiftly zigzagged toward the bridge, only the deep rattle of burp guns and the crack of rifle fire challenged them. And, while several GIs fell wounded, the bulk of Wittig's troops reached the north end of the bridge and sent streams of fire into the Germans defenders. The heavy assault wounded three Germans and killed four more, including Lt. Heinz Becker. The 7th Parachute Division cadre leader had caught two hits in the stomach that almost tore out his insides with a gush of blood. Becker doubled over and then toppled off the bridge and fell into the water of the canal with a heavy splash.

Captain Wilhelm Geyer, meanwhile, caught a hit in the right thigh and the sting prompted him to grimace in agony. His legs caved in and he collapsed to the deck of the bridge. When he finally looked up, four American soldiers were standing over him with aimed weapons.

Geyer forced a grin. "Aufgeben!" he said softly.

The 2nd Battalion commander stared about the area and then pursed his lips in dismay. His troops had been thoroughly routed, there was no doubt of that, and the bridges were now in American hands. He felt a sympathy for Colonel Ross and his Volkstrum troops inside of Wesel. With the canal cut off, Geyer doubted that Ross and his men could hold out long. He hoped the rest of his battalion, those on the dams to the east, would have better luck.

But the German troops on the two dams, about two miles east of these captured bridges, suffered the same routing defeat. Col. Jim Pierce approached the dams with more than 500 men. Also with him were six Sherman tanks and eight 105mm mobile guns. The colonel peered carefully through field glasses to study the German positions. Like Captain Wittig, Pierce also wanted these dams intact. As a matter of fact, he did not even order fire on the dams, but called for air support. He wanted the Germans to think they were undergoing air attacks and not ground attacks. Pierce hoped to get his men within point blank range of the dams, while the Germans sheltered themselves from the air assaults. The 194th Regiment commander could then perhaps overrun the German defenders before the enemy destroyed the dams or opened the locks.

At 1500 hours, a squadron of P-47s roared over the Issel Canal dams to unleash rocket and machine gun fire. As expected, the Germans sheltered themselves during the attack that continued for ten minutes, while Pierce brought his troops and armor almost to the foot of the dams. By the time the P-47s had soared away, Pierce opened with machine guns, bazookas, and light artillery from the Sherman tanks.

The Germans, not yet regrouped from the aerial attacks, offered only a haphazard, confused resistance. Before they could wreck the dams, the GIs swarmed over the catwalks, unleashing heavy fire ahead of them, and pushed the Germans to the south end of the dams. In less than a half hour, Pierce captured both dams intact, while his GIs killed 31 soldiers of the German 2nd Battalion and captured nearly 50 more. The others had successfully escaped the Americans and hurried eastward to Gahlen.

Jim Pierce then contacted Captain Wittig and the colonel was delighted to learn that the C Company commander had seized the bridges intact. "Nice work, Captain. We've got the canal effectively cut off and use of the bridges. The Germans can't get a goddamn thing into the city over this waterway."

Pierce also learned that the other battalions of

the 194th Regiment had successfully struck the defenses on the Issel River and chased off the Germans who had hurried off to the northeast. But even more important, these elements of the 194th had linked up with British 7th Division troops to the northward.

However, Pierce got an ominous call from Gen. Bud Miley, commander of the 17th Airborne Division. "Colonel, strengthen your positions along the river and the canal. Intelligence tells us that large units of the German 15th Panzer Division are just east of you. They may try to break through and retake those dams and bridges."

"Yes sir."

Meanwhile the other groups of men from the 194th were still plodding south and southwest. S/Sgt. Tom Martin, as he moved, saw his ranks swell to almost 50 men as GIs, two TDs, and two mobile artillery crews joined him. The motley force did not really know where they were going except that the Issel Canal objective was in a southerly direction. As they marched, Martin and his dogfaces spent most of their time clearing small German pockets of resistance.

In one skirmish, Cpl. Homer Moyer, a medic, had been captured as he attempted to reach a wounded man. However, his captors had later come under heavy attack by a British unit, and the Germans saw the hopelessness of further resistance. Yet they did not know how to give themselves up and they asked Corporal Moyer to take them in.

"We will not harm you."

Moyer grinned. Then with one of the Germans' own weapons to guard the accommodating enemy troops, the medic lined up the 20 Germans in a column of twos and marched them to the British lines. "I've got a bunch of prisoners for you. Don't shoot!"

The British were astonished to see the parade of surrendering Germans, accompanied by a single guard with a German weapon. "Blimey," one of the Tommies gaped, "did you ever see a bloody thing like that?"

By nightfall, Sergeant Martin had reached the CP of Colonel Pierce's 194th Regiment along the Issel Canal. He had with him more than 30 prisoners and about 10 wounded GIs. Captain Wittig warmly greeted his sergeant. "I'm glad you caught up to us, especially with all these stragglers. We were afraid you and the others were dead or prisoners."

"We did our best, sir," Martin said.

The captain nodded. "We're camping here for the night and we'll try to get those from other companies back to their units in the morning."

"What about our objective?"

Wittig grinned. "You're a little late, Sergeant. We took the bridges a couple of hours ago, and the other battalions took the dams to the east."

Meanwhile, Lt. Col. Joe Keating of the 681st Glider Artillery was also coming south with his big mobile guns, some Sherman tanks, Lieutenant Richey, Sergeant Woolfort, and other stragglers from the 194th and 681st. The motley unit had spent most of their time clearing German pockets in their path.

As the column moved south, a column of 150 Germans, with tanks and self-propelled guns broke out of a patch of woods and attacked Keating's troops. But the lieutenant colonel sent his men to cover and then ordered his 105 mobile guns and Sherman tanks to disperse.

The GIs dove off the opposite side of the road and into ditches, while the mobile vehicles veered left and right. Thus two volleys of German shells failed to hit the Americans. Keating peered through his field glasses and watched the Germans emerge from some trees. Wehrmacht soldiers were following the armor and the Germans apparently hoped to run over the Americans with their tanks and self-propelled guns. But Keating waited patiently and ordered the 105mm and tank teams to aim their guns across the road. The colonel waited until the rumbling Mark IVs and artillery came within almost to the opposite side of the road. Then he cried to his gunners.

"Fire!"

A barrage of 105 and 75 shells struck the Germans from almost point blank range, so close that GIs cowered deep in the ravines to avoid falling shrapnel. More than 20 shells ripped into the advancing Germans and within moments, Keating's assault had killed 50 Germans, knocked out three tanks, and all of the self-propelled guns. The other Germans scattered back into the trees.

Keating continued on with his mixed bag of

GIs, tanks, and mobile guns. He had moved another mile when survivors of the German unit attempted to attack him again. But once more, the Wehrmacht troops were cut down by cannon, BAR, and machine gun fire. Only 30 of the Germans had survived their two attempted attacks and they surrendered in the obviously useless cause.

But Keating's odyssey was not yet over. Less than a mile south he ran into a vacant farmhouse where several GIs had rushed inside to take advantage of whatever comforts they might find here. The soldiers found wine, soft beds, and a soft divan to rest and relax, much to the chagrin of the GIs left outside during a ten minute break.

As the gloating GIs enjoyed their finds inside the farmhouse, a trio of ME 110 light German bombers attempted to support some troops on the Issel Canal. But a swarm of American P-38s quickly shot down all three. One of the ME 110s, smoking badly, crashed within a few yards of the farmhouse, exploding in a ball of fire and smoke. The GIs inside suddenly saw their comfort turn to near disaster. They rushed headlong out of the building, stumbling and falling as they ran. Luckily, none of the men had been killed and they drew laughter and jokes from the GIs who had been denied the same luxury inside the house.

Keating's force moved on and by dark, they too had reached the CP of the 194th Regiment. Here, Col. Jim Pierce welcomed Keating and relieved the 681st commander of his many prisoners.

"Camp your men here for the night," Pierce said.

"Which way do we go then?" the 681st Artillery commander asked.

Pierce shrugged. "I don't know. Division says the Germans are mustering for a counterattack. I guess G-2 wants to wait for reconnaissance reports. We may help them clear Wesel or we might go east to meet any German attack."

Lt. Col. Joe Keating nodded.

Thus by the end of this first day, the Americans had made considerable progress. In fact, the U.S. troops had gained more than expected, despite the heavy German assault against the descending parachutes and gliders.

The Germans, in fact, were in a precarious position. The 30th U.S. Infantry Division had reached its objective on the Lippe River, particularly the 120th Regiment under Col. Branner Purdue who had cleared Schanzenberg. The 513th and 507th Regiments of the 17th Airborne had cleared the entire area between Hamminkeln and Wesel, capturing Hamminkeln, Diersfordt, and Platte. The 194th Glider Regiment had taken key positions on the Issel Canal and Issel River, while the American 79th Infantry Division had captured Dinslaken south of Wesel.

Most of the German troops of General Gericke's 2nd Parachute Division and General Waldenburg's 116th Greyhound Panzer Division had fled eastward, leaving Colonel Ross's Wesel Division trapped inside the battered Rhine city.

Help could not reach the Volkstrum troops and Ross would fight a desperate battle while he waited for reinforcements from Army Group H to break through and relieve him.

And, in fact, Field Marshal Johannes Blaskowitz had been amassing troops of the 5th Panzer Division at Borken, some 25 miles northeast of Wesel, while elements of both the 2nd Parachute and 116th Panzer Divisions had retreated into Hunxe to regroup. Further, another regiment of the 84th Division had mustered at Gahlen, 20 miles east of Wesel. But could these units of the German Army Group H stem the advance of the U.S. 17th Airborne, 30th Infantry, and 79th Infantry Divisions?

CHAPTER TWELVE

In the village of Schanzenberg on the Lippe River, dawn of 25 March broke clear and dry. Col. Branner Purdue of the 30th Infantry's 120th Regiment was already awake and discussing strategy with his battalion commanders, Lt. Col. Ed Cantey and Lt. Col. Bud Williamson. Purdue spread a map on the table and tapped a point with a pencil.

"Right here, Kirchhellen; as soon as more armor and mobile guns get here, we'll move southeast in force. The 117th Regiment will attack Hunxe and our job is to take Kirchhellen. We've got reports the Germans are reinforcing that village, bringing in troops to both Hunxe and Kirchhellen from the east."

"The enemy's been tough so far, Colonel,"

Cantey said.

"It doesn't matter," the 120th Regiment commander answered. "That's our objective, and I'd like to secure Kirchhellen by nightfall."

By the time the sun rose from the east, T/Sgt. Harry Boures was fully dressed and he moved among the G Company campsite to awaken his men of 2nd Platoon. "Okay, shake it up! Let's go!"

The GIs responded, leaving their pup tents and quickly washing as best they could in their helmets before they walked through a chow line where company cooks offered them coffee and heated C rations, their first hot meal in nearly 36 hours. The men appreciated the fare because they were hungry and even these simple rations were a welcome change from K ration.

The GIs had just finished breakfast when a line of tanks growled through the rubbled streets of Schanzenberg in a zigzagging column. The tank commander immediately met with Branner Purdue.

"How many tanks do you have?" the colonel asked.

"Twenty-six Shermans, along with 90mm guns."

"Good," Purdue nodded. He looked at his watch. "We'll be moving out at 0800 and we should reach Kirchhellen in about two or three hours. I'll call for air support to give the town a working over before we attack,"

"Yes sir," the tank commander said.

But then the two officers stiffened and

frowned when they heard the high pitched whines in the sky, a sound they had never heard before. Purdue squinted upward and saw the formations of dark shapes to the north. He, the battalion commanders, and the tank unit major then watched the shapes loom large until they saw clearly aircraft with pods under their wings instead of propellers and motors.

"Goddamn it, Colonel," Ed Cantey gaped, "They're jet planes!"

Purdue jerked and then shouted frantically. "Take cover! Pass the word to take cover."

Within a minute, the order had spread throughout the battered town of Schanzenberg, where the GIs had bivouacked for the night after capturing the town. Purdue, meanwhile, quickly called 30th Division headquarters.

"We've got jets coming over. Get a CAP here to intercept right away."

"Okay, Colonel," somebody answered.

In the sky, Lt. Col. Johannes Steinhoff, in the lead ME 262 twin engine jet fighter bomber, peered down at the sprawling patch of terrain ahead until he saw the winding Lippe River and the battered buildings of Schanzenberg. Steinhoff was leading 16 ME 262s, each carrying a quartet of 400 kg bombs as well as rockets. He called his fellow pilots.

"We will make our attack in three aircraft waves." Then, Steinhoff led the first line of planes into the village, unleashing rocket fire from 500 yards before unleashing the whistling bombs.

The streaming rockets exploded amid the rubbled town, knocking down scarred walls, erupting more debris in the streets, hitting some of the American foxholes, igniting vehicles, and knocking out three of the tanks that had just arrived. Then came the bombs that ignited more U.S. vehicles, shattered several more foxholes, and turned three more tanks into flaming wrecks.

In his foxhole, Sgt. Harry Boures, Cpl. Les Belden, and Pvt. Earl Otto cowered in fear as the exploding rockets and bombs shook the ground, bouncing the GIs, while the staccato of blasts nearly deafened them. They expected at any moment to meet sudden death. The strange, screaming pitch of jet engines, totally alien, rattled the soldiers even more than the exploding shells. They shuddered at the sight of the streaking jets that zoomed over them in fleeting seconds.

"Goddamn, Sarge," Private Otto cursed, "where the hell's our fighter cover? Why aren't they hittin' those planes with ack ack?"

"Shit," Belden cursed, "those jets are too fast. The AA gunners don't even have time to aim and our fighter planes could never catch 'em."

The G Company soldiers cowered again as another sextet of 400 kg bombs from more jets exploded in Schanzenberg.

Finally, the ME 262s were gone, fading quickly and disappearing to dots, while their screaming engines diminished to waning echoes. As the GIs crawled nervously out of their shelters, they stared at the countless fires and palls of smoke about them. Six tanks, two mobile guns, and about a dozen trucks burned furiously from the rocket or bomb hits. About 30 GIs had died, their bodies riddled with shrapnel from the numbing air attack. Some were buried under rubble like distorted, discarded mannequins in a refuse dump. Damage and casualties had been heavy, but Colonel Purdue was determined to move ahead.

"We took some bad hits," the 120th Regiment colonel told his officers, "but they certainly didn't put us out of business." He looked at an aide. "Get this mess cleared and take care of casualties. We'll be moving out at 0800 as scheduled."

"Yes sir," the captain said.

Then as the men mustered, the whine of planes echoed in the sky. A squadron of P-38s had arrived over Schanzenberg. Private Otto scowled.

"Now the bastards show up."

"It wouldn't have made any difference," Sergeant Boures said. "They'd never have caught those jets, anyway."

The P-38 fighter planes circled and arched about the sky, but the pilots had seen no sign of the Luftwaffe attackers. In fleeting moments, the ME 262s had reached the American positions, made their attacks, and zoomed off. Purdue asked the P-38 squadron leader to stay close because his regiment and the attached tank unit was moving out to Kirchhellen.

"We don't want any more of those goddamn air attacks," Purdue said, "especially on the open roads."

"We'll hang upstairs as long as we can, Colonel," the squadron leader said.

On schedule, at 0800 hours, the Americans moved out of Schanzenberg to roll toward Kirchhellen, 80 miles to the southeast.

At the same early morning hour, 25 March, American troops of the 513th Parachute Regiment at Platte met the same fearful air attack as did the troops of the U.S. 120th Regiment at Schanzenberg. The soldiers of Lieutenant Colonel Miller's 2nd Battalion had just left their bivouac tents where they had slept for the night, when they heard the sound of strange engines in the sky. They had never known anything like this before and they peered at the approaching dots to the northeast. Soon, they saw the shapes of alien aircraft with hanging pods under the wings instead of prop engines. They had not realized the aircraft were AR 234 twin engine jet bombers.

As the sixteen light bombers from KG 51 under Maj. Walter Kowakoski roared toward Platte, the 2nd Battalion GIs stood immobile and stared at the strange planes. After the first three bombers whooshed over Platte with blinding speed, the American soldiers gawked. But then, as whooshing 400 kg bombs exploded off to the left, the GIs scattered quickly for cover, jumping into shell craters, bomb craters, or abandoned German bunkers.

Lieutenant Colonel Miller frantically wound his field telephone and called 17th Division headquarters. "They're bombing us with those new jets. Where the hell is our fighter cover?"

"They're supposed to be out there, Colonel."

Miller cowered and closed his eyes as another sextet of bombs from three more AR 234s struck Platte in a staccato of b-blooms that erupted clods of earth and debris. Particles of earth bounced off Miller's steel helmet and he hugged the ground. Seconds later, he screamed into his field telephone. "Get those goddamn fighter planes here. How the hell come they let those jets hit us?"

"I'll do what I can, sir."

As Miller slammed down the phone, he cowered still again as yet more AR 234s streaked over Platte and dropped six more bombs that rocked the crossroad village just north of Wesel. This time, one bomb hit squarely on a shell crater that sheltered six GIs and blew the half dozen American soldiers to shreds. A second bomb struck next to a TD and the explosion turned the vehicle into a ball of fire. A third bomb struck a mobile 105mm gun and literally lifted the heavy artillery piece several feet off the ground before the gun fell to earth in a mangled mass of steel.

Miller again called division headquarters. "Goddamn it, get those fighter planes over here."

"Yes sir," the headquarters aide said.

Less than a hundred yards from their battalion commander, S/Sgt. John Queenan, Private Hines, Private Leonard, and Private Walley cowered in a huge shell hole where a rain of earth had dropped into their shelter after a bomb explosion. The jet bombers rocketing overhead had terrified them even more than the bombs themselves.

"Goddamn it, Sarge," Private Hines hissed, "did you ever see anything like that? Anything like that?"

"They're goin' by like fuckin' meteors," Private Walley said. "How can they make anything that flies so fast?"

"How the hell should I know," Queenan answered.

Then the four soldiers cowered again as another trio of twin engine jets whooshed across the sky and dropped another six 400 kg bombs. Once more a staccato of explosions caused death and damage. Another shell crater, also crowded with GIs, erupted from a numbing blast that ripped to death the four soldiers inside. Another TD went up in smoke, another gun was smashed, and another building flattened.

Meanwhile, Col. George Bickel had received the call from 17th Airborne headquarters. "A bunch of German jets are plastering our position in Platte. We're going over to intercept," he told his pilots. The 354th Fighter Group commander, whose 24 P-47s were on CAP, then veered southeast and roared toward Platte. The colonel soon observed the streaking, black painted jets that were zooming over the village in three plane Vs. Bickel was awed by the speed of these aircraft, but he was determined to break up the attack.

"Hit them in pairs, in pairs," Bickel cried.

"We hear you, Colonel," Maj. John Howard answered.

The P-47s then peeled off and dove toward the German jet bombers. Among Major Kowakoski's 16 jet bombers, 12 of them had already made their runs over Platte, causing serious but not fatal damage. One of the German pilots spotted the American fighter planes and he quickly called his kommandant.

"Major, enemy fighter planes at two o'clock, high."

"I am sure you can complete your bombing attack before they reach you," Kowakoski said.

"But they will pursue us and their fighters are more maneuverable than our bombers."

"It does not matter," the KG 51 commander answered. "You need only climb away and speed back to base."

"Yes, Herr Major."

And in fact, the last four planes in the German formation did zoom over Platte and drop their bombs before Bickel and his P-47 pilots could stop them. The last series of explosions killed or injured another dozen GIs and destroyed two more armored vehicles. As the American fighter planes took after the twin engine jets, the GIs emerged shakily from their shelters amid the fire and smoke in the village, and they watched the P-47 pursuit. However, both the American soldiers and pilots gaped at the amazing speed of the AR 234s.

Major Kowakoski had ordered his Luftwaffe pilots to climb away from the American fighter planes and speed back to base. The sixteen AR 234 bombers had zoomed upward in the sky at incredible speed, well over 600 MPH, climbing to 20,000 feet. The jet bombers had then jelled into formation and whined northeastward at a dizzy pace. Within two minutes they lost sight of the P-47s.

Bickel simply gawked, sighed, and then called his pilots. "We'll never catch them. Break off pursuit and maintain CAP over Platte for the time being."

"Yes sir," Maj. Jim Howard said.

On the ground, in the battered village of Platte, the GIs of the 513th Parachute Regiment had watched the events in the sky with astonishment. They had seen dogfights in the past between American and Luftwaffe fighters where the U.S. pilots had usually caught up with the German ME 109 and FW 190 conventional aircraft, especially with P-51s. But this sight had been incredible. The German jets had made their runs and disappeared, leaving behind the pursuing P-47s as greyhounds might leave behind lumbering crustaceans.

"Son of a bitch," Private Hines cursed. "We ain't got a chance against them jets; not a chance."

"Not unless we keep planes over us all the time," Private Leonard said as he squinted up at the loitering Thunderbolts.

"Well, we got one break," Sergeant Queenan said. "They don't have too many of those things. They ain't likely to come back today. If they go back to their bases and load up again, they'll probably try to hit somebody else."

"I hope so," Private Hines said.

While the GIs of the 120th and 513th American Regiments still trembled from the jet air attacks, all was quiet about the 194th Regiment encampment around the Issel Canal bridges, northeast of Wesel. Col. Jim Pierce of the glider regiment and Col. Joe Keating of the 681st Glider Artillery had also risen early to plan their next move. The two men sat in a tent headquarters with Captain Wittig of C Company, Captain Lyerly of E Company, and Captain Dukes of F Company. Only moments before the meeting on this early morning of 25 March, Pierce had received a communication from the 17th Airborne headquarters:

"Leave a force to hold the canal bridges and move the remainder of your force to the eastward to join the attack on Wesel. Col. James Morrisey of the Canadian 1st Commando Brigade will join the 194th Regiment to clear the northern sector of the city."

Colonel Pierce read the directive to the assembled officers and then gestured. "It's obvious they're using other units of our divisions to move north and east to link up with British forces and our ground troops that are moving south and east. I guess they want Wesel cleared as soon as possible and the more troops and armor we have for the job, the better."

"That makes sense, Colonel," Captain Wittig said.

"I expect to meet with Colonel Morrisey in about an hour, and we'll plan a twin drive through the northern areas of Wesel. That means a lot of house to house fighting if the Germans offer stiff resistance. But with armor support, the job should go easier." He looked at Keating. "Colonel?"

The 681st commander referred to a sheet in his hand before he spoke. "Most of my regimental units have pretty well organized themselves by now. I have one battalion of tanks and mobile artillery joining the 513th at Platte and the other battalions are coming here to join us. They've got about thirty Shermans, thirty TD's and at least twenty mobile guns. But," he gestured, "if we're heading for Wesel, I'll tell them to alter their route and meet us east of here."

"Good idea," Pierce nodded. "I'd like to have a company of artillery and a half dozen TDs with my battalion that remains here on the Issel Canal locks and bridges. If the Germans are massing more troops at Borken to the northeast, and if they break through the British units, they may try to take the canal positions. My battalion will certainly need armor and artillery support."

"Okay, Jim," Keating answered Pierce.

The 194th commander then sighed. "Okay, get back to your units. As soon as the men finish breakfast, we'll move east, probably at 0800. Meanwhile, I'll contact Colonel Morrisey of the Canadians and determine where we might link up."

In the bivouac area, Sgt. William Woolfort,

Sgt. Clint Hedrick, Sgt. Tom Martin, and other non-coms rousted GIs from their pup tent shelters. "Okay, up and out, up and out!" The shouts of sergeants echoed throughout the wide patch of terrain where the tired GIs had slept for the night after a busy day yesterday. As the men moved through chow lines to eat hot C rations, they grumbled in disappointment. They had hoped that supply trucks had brought in something more palatable for the morning meal.

Sergeant Woolfort and Sergeant Hedrick sat on a patch of ground to eat their breakfast.

"Where are we going from here?" Woolfort asked.

"I heard a rumor early this morning from a guy in the CP," Hedrick said. "They say we're going west to join the Canadians to take Wesel."

"Christ, I thought that was a whole British deal."

"No," Hedrick said. "Our own 30th Infantry guys are fighting in the southern part of Wesel. I guess we and the Canadians will take the northern end."

Sergeant Woolfort squinted up at the clear morning sky and then looked at the terrain to the east, a mixture of pasture lands and forest, the same kind of terrain they had passed since they landed in the rickety gliders. "Goddamn," he said, "I hope we don't run into a hundred pockets of krauts between here and Wesel like we did yesterday."

Hedrick shrugged. "I got a suspicion we won't. They must know we're heading for Wesel and that we'll have plenty of armor with us. I'd guess they'll move every gun and every man they can into Wesel to defend the city."

"That'll mean heavy house to house fighting," Woolfort said.

By 0800 hours, the long stream of TDs, Sherman tanks, and mobile guns, carrying GI passengers, began moving westward. They had come within a mile of Wesel without encountering enemy resistance before Col. Jim Pierce held up the column and met with his commanders.

"Our sector is here on the northeast quadrant of Wesel, and the Canadians will be hitting the northwest quadrant. We'll launch our first attack as soon as the armor joins us. Then we'll work our way through the city until we link up with the Canadians."

"Yes sir," Captain Wittig said.

At Schanzenberg, despite the Luftwaffe jet air attack, Col. Branner Purdue mustered his troops of the 120th Infantry Regiment to march southeast toward Schanzenberg. By 0900 hours, Purdue's infantrymen, with an attached battalion of armor, had begun rolling toward Kirchhellen.

At Platte, after the bomber attack, Col. Jim Coutts readied his 513th Regiment and then met with his officers. "I know that goddamn jet bomber attack was a hell of a way to start a morning, but we still have a job to do. Anyway, we didn't suffer that badly. Lucky for us, they don't have too many jets."

"No sir," the diminutive Lt. Col. Allen Miller said.

Coutts spread a map on a table and then pointed to an area running eastward. "We'll be joining the Canadian 6th Brigade for a twin drive eastward. The Canadians will follow the highway and we'll follow the railroad pike. We're going all the way to Dorsten—beyond the autobahn. We might run into trouble here, at Gahlen, but we'll just have to clear any resistance we might find there and keep moving. By this time tomorrow we should occupy our objective."

"What about the junction here at Platte?" Miller asked.

"Elements of the 507th Regiment will hold here and they might join other units in the fight for Wesel."

Miller nodded.

"Okay, assemble your men; give them breakfast and mount them up."

And finally, west of the Issel Canal bridges, Col. Jim Pierce and his mixed trooper-armor unit was well on the way to Wesel. He would stop only to meet the 681st Glider Artillery along the way.

The Germans, of course, had not been idle during the dark hours of 24-25 March. Field Marshal Blaskowitz had been awake throughout the night, while he discussed strategy with his commanders. By daylight, his intelligence reports had pretty well confirmed the expected movements of the Allied forces that had breached the Rhine by water and by air. The Army Group H commander had alerted the troops of the 15th Panzer Division at Borken, 25 miles northeast of Wesel, and these troops would attempt to hold off and even repel British troops who were moving swiftly northeastward from their landing areas above Hamminkeln.

Blaskowitz had also ordered strong defenses established at Hunxe, east of Wesel, and at Gahlen and Dorsten further east. Finally, he ordered the merging troops in Kirchhellen to hold firm and he ordered the troops in Wesel to fight to the death to hold the city.

"Are all defenses in order?" Blaskowitz asked his commanders.

"Elements of the 2nd Parachute Division's FJR 6 and the 116th Panzer's 60th Regiment have retired to reform at Kirchhellen," General Schlemm of the 1st Parachute Army said. "Both Colonel Heydte and Colonel Harzer have assured us that they have established strong defenses. I have also been assured that our jet air units will give us air support wherever needed."

"Good," the field marshal said.

General Schlemm then pawed through more papers on his desk. "A full regiment of the 84th Division has set up defenses at Gahlen, and a battalion of armor from the 15th Panzer has been rushed to join General Craseman's 84th Division troops at Gahlen. I understand that they have also manned secondary defenses at Dorsten to the east." The general shook his head. "As for Wesel, Herr Field Marshal, I do not know what is to happen there."

"Unfortunately, Colonel Ross finds himself in a most dangerous position," Blaskowitz said.

"He is now all but surrounded by enemy forces with little prospect of getting reinforcements. Still, he has a formidable force within the city with substantial guns. He must hold the city to the last man. General Wilke has assured me that the KG 51 jet bomber units will begin making strikes on Allied troops concentrations this morning and they will continue their air support duties for the remainder of the day, especially in Wesel."

"Let us hope we do better today than we did yesterday," Schlemm said.

If the Germans had taken a bad beating on 24 March, they intended to redeem themselves on this 25 March. At Kirchhellen, Col. Friherr von der Heydte kept men posted to keep a sharp lookout to the west. Soon enough, American troops of the 120th Regiment would come into view. Further north, at Gahlen, General Craseman's 84th Division troops kept similar lookouts to watch the roads and railroad pike running east from Wesel to Dorsten. Here too, Wehrmacht sentinels would soon enough see the approaching GIs of the 513th Parachute Regiment. And finally, in Wesel itself, Col. Frederick Ross mustered the troops of his Wesel Volkstrum Division for a last ditch stand. He had placed artillery pieces and machine gun nests at strategic locations, especially to the east. Before long, the GIs of the 194th Glider Regiment would clash head on with these Volkstrum defenders.

Thus, heavy fighting would erupt again on the second day of Operation Plunder.

CHAPTER THIRTEEN

Col. Branner Purdue's column of the 120th Regiment dogfaces and accompanying armor moved southeast with few initial problems. His troops rode leisurely atop the tanks and TDs and hope grew that perhaps the Germans had abandoned Kirchhellen and the Americans could take this objective with little difficulty. However, at Hunxe, along the Lippe-Seiten Canal, the 30th Division's 117th Regiment had run into heavy resistance and they would need a full day to clear the enemy here. So Purdue most likely would meet the same kind of resistance at his own target.

In fact, hordes of Germans had moved into Kirchhellen and set up defenses along the Dinslaken-Kirchhellen Highway. Colonel Heydte had established his headquarters in the town, directing the combined remnants of his own FJR 6 and the 60th Regiments. Heydte had amassed more than a 1,000 foot soldiers, along with 15 halftracks armed with 20mm anti-aircraft guns, six 76mm artillery pieces, six 90mm pieces, three ammo trucks, and a horde of motor vehicles that included ten Mark IV medium tanks. The FJR 6 colonel prepared to throw this weight against any attacking Americans.

When the 120th came within two miles of Kirchhellen, Colonel Purdue established a unit called Hunt Force, an infantry-tank force that combined the 2nd Battalion infantrymen and the 823rd Battalion TDs. At 1215 hours, immediately after the noon meal, Purdue ordered this force, under the command of Lt. Col. Richard Hunt of the 823rd, to spearhead the drive into Kirchhellen. As the Americans neared a wooded area, about a mile from the town, an eruption of 76mm and 90mm German fire spewed out of the woods. The abrupt shelling chopped huge holes in the terrain and numbed the GIs. Three TDs burst into flames from direct hits, while the same numbing blasts killed 16 GIs and wounded several more.

The Americans scattered to shelter themselves, as rattling machine gun fire also poured out of the woodlands. T/Sgt. Harry Boures, along with Pvt. Earl Otto and Cpl. Les Belden, dove into a hole.

"Son of a bitch," Otto cursed. "Those woods are crawling with the bastards."

"Those goddamn krauts ain't never gonna quit," Cpl. Les Belden complained.

"What are we gonna do?" Otto asked Boures.

"I don't know," the sergeant answered. "I'd guess we'll hit them back with our own artillery and maybe with fighter bombers. Then we'll have to clear the bitches out of the woods."

"Shit," Belden cursed again, "we'll never finish this job; never."

The three men cowered again as more 76mm shells exploded nearby, vibrating the ground with numbing blasts that almost deafened the 2nd Battalion trio.

Colonel Von der Heydte had prepared well, leaving the 60th Grenadier Regiment of mixed armor, artillery, and foot soldiers in the wooded areas east of Kirchhellen. Col. Walter Harzer himself directed this force against the oncoming Americans, and his unit had scored the initial blow.

Col. Branner Purdue quickly asked for air support, while he ordered his own tanks forward. He then called for a counter barrage from his 90mm mobile field guns. Less than two minutes after the Germans launched their own attack, the Americans responded in kind. 75mm tank guns and heavy 105mm field guns sent arching shells into the woods. Erupting explosions, balls of fire, and heavy palls of smoke soon rose from the patch of forest. Now the Germans scurried for cover.

For nearly ten minutes American shells pounded the German positions. Then, a squadron of P-47 fighter-bombers arrived in the area. In pairs, the Thunderbolts zoomed over the forest to unleash whooshing 5″ incendiary rockets and whistling 250 pound demolition bombs. A staccato of numbing explosions shook the brake before a new mass of fire and smoke rose out of the trees.

Private Otto and Corporal Belden rose from their shell hole to view the burning woodlands. "Christ," Otto hissed. "That goddamn attack must have burned every kraut inside those trees."

"There can't be many of the bastards left," Corporal Belden nodded.

In fact, the Germans *had* suffered heavy casualties. Nearly 100 soldiers had been seared to death from the raging woodland fires ignited by the American artillery and aircraft attacks. The assault had also destroyed four half tracks and damaged four, while destroying two 76mm and 90mm gun emplacements. Then one of the ammunition trucks caught a hit and exploded in a numbing blast that echoed as far as two miles away. Col. Walter Harzer ordered a retreat from the burning woods since the forest had obviously become untenable. The 60th Regiment commander would only lose more of his troops and equipment if he remained here.

But Lieutenant Colonel Hunt took advantage of the diminished German fire by quickly circumventing the burning patch of trees with his armor and the 2nd Battalion troops to cut off the retreating Germans. The GIs and their TDs were on the other side of the forest just as the Germans were pulling out of the conflagration.

"Fire!" Hunt cried.

A volley of 75mm TD shells pummelled the enemy troops, annihilating 15 or 20 Wehrmacht soldiers before the others retreated back into the burning trees. Then 75mm guns from the 823rd TD Battalion continued to pelt the Germans, while U.S. infantry troops quickly dismounted and pursued the Germans to the edge of the woodland. The 60th Regiment troops were now trapped between the raging forest fires behind them and the American Hunt Force in front of them.

T/Sgt. Harry Boures took his platoon and crossed the open ground between the road and flaming forest, but he and several GIs suddenly froze and hugged the ground when German machine gunners sent withering streams of fire into the American ranks.

"Holy Christ," one of Boures' men hissed, "they'll get us for sure out here in the open. Can you call for artillery support?"

"We're too close," Boures said. "Cover me."

"What are you gonna do?"

"Get those goddamn krauts before they get us."

"But, Sarge—"

"Cover me!" Boures barked sharply.

The platoon sergeant leaped to his feet and zigzagged forward, avoiding the pops of earth that erupted from the machine gun bullets. He returned a spew of slugs from his blazing BAR, firing from the hip. His men watched in awe, as the sergeant raced forward for an astonishing 75 yards without getting hit. He reached the gun emplacement and unleashed another rattle of BAR fire that chopped away chunks of earth from the bank sheltering the machine gunners. The gunners inside cowered and then ducked as a 75mm shell whizzed over their heads and exploded behind them. Finally, a white handkerchief fluttered above the machine gun position.

"Kommen aus!" Boures cried.

Four Germans then surrendered meekly to the platoon sergeant.

Meanwhile, Pfc. Earl Otto conducted his own private war. He quickly loaded a drum into his own BAR and crawled forward toward another machine gun nest that had also raked more advancing 2nd Battalion GIs. Otto only needed two minutes to come within 10 yards of the German nest. He then quickly rose to his feet and hurled a grenade that landed squarely inside the enemy position before the nest exploded. The three men in the position died instantly.

"Come on you guys, come on," Otto waved to his fellow GIs.

A dozen dogfaces leaped to their feet and rushed forward to join Otto. The soldiers then darted into the woods and opened fire on anything that moved. Within moments, they flushed out nearly 50 German prisoners.

Now with the machine gun positions silent, Lt. Col. Ed Cantey gestured to his dogfaces of 2nd Battalion to hurry forward, while Lieutenant Colonel Hunt pushed on his TDs that had fired more 75mm shells and rattling machinegun fire into the woods. The exploding shells knocked down trees, shattered limbs, and destroyed more of the 60th Grenadier armor inside.

The Germans, now in a helpless position, began to surrender in droves. Within a half hour, 655 Germans came out of the woods to give up. Among them was the 60th Regiment commander, Col. Walter Harzer. Only Maj. Sepp Krafft and a few others had escaped back to Kirchhellen. The elite 60th Grenadier Regiment of the famed 116th Panzer Greyhound Division had been annihilated.

Col. Branner Purdue wasted no time. After clearing the woods, he quickly reformed his men, armor, and guns. But 1400 hours, the Americans were rumbling toward Kirchhellen. But once more the U.S. column came under attack. Within a mere 100 yards of the village, an eruption of tank fire and 88mm artillery fire came from the town.

The Americans dove into ditches on both sides of the road, while their TDs zigzagged in several directions to avoid exploding Germans shells. Colonel von der Heydte, despite the loss of the 60th Grenadiers, was not ready to give up. In fact, he had audaciously launched a counterattack out of Kirchhellen against the Americans. Several Mark IVs led the way, with hordes of FJR 6 paratroops following behind the tanks.

Heavy 76mm fire boomed from the barrels of the Panthers, forcing the Americans to retreat. The TDs, despite their numbers, were really no match for the Panzer medium tank. But Colonel Purdue quickly used his advantage that was not available to the Germans—air power. The 120th Regiment commander again called for air support.

Moments later, a squadron of P-47s once more reached the area. The Thunderbolts peeled off and dove into the German tank column, unleashing whooshing 5″ rockets and numbing 250 pound bombs. The attack knocked out three Mark IVs and damaged two more. The same assault also knocked out two 88mm guns. The German troops and surviving tanks scurried in several directions to avoid destruction.

As soon as the U.S. P-47s broke up the German counter attack, Colonel Purdue pushed his men and armor forward and by late in the day they reached the battered village of Kirchhellen. U.S. 75mm and 105mm artillery then shelled the German positions inside the town.

But still, during the waning afternoon, the Germans continued to fight vigorously. However, G and E Company of Lieutenant Colonel Cantey's 2nd Battalion fought just as hard. Before nightfall, Sgt. Harry Boures led a platoon of men through some of the rubbled streets until they came close to a tank, whose idling engine sputtered in coughing pops. A squad of German troops were loitering behind the Mark IV and Boures called on Earl Otto who approached the tank with a bazooka. Otto took careful aim and fired two shells into the Panther, striking the vulnerable neck of the turret. Both shells exploded, setting the tank afire.

Before the German crew or the Wehrmacht soldiers reacted to the sudden attack, Boures and his platoon fired a heavy fusillade of BAR and rifle fire into the German ranks. Several of the enemy soldiers fell and the others quickly surrendered. "Aufgeben! Aufgeben!"

For the rest of the day, and well into the evening, the GIs from the 120th Regiment and 823rd TD Battalion fought their way through the rubbled streets of Kirchhellen, killing more Germans, destroying more trucks, and taking more prisoners. At 2100 hours, Colonel Purdue threw more TDs and mobile artillery into the fight and before another hour passed, the GIs had cleared the rest of the town. At 2200 hours, Colonel Purdue, Lieutenant Colonel Cantey, and Lieutenant Colonel Hunt stood on a knoll east of the town and looked down at the autobahn in the distance. They did not see a single German soldier, not one piece of armor, and no planes; nothing at all.

"I guess we'll make it, Colonel," Cantey said.

"We've taken over fifteen hundred prisoners, sir," Hunt said.

Purdue nodded. "They're finished. We've cleared a path into the heart of the Ruhr."

"What do we do now, sir?" Hunt asked.

"Bed down the troops for the night," the 120th Regiment commander said. "This thing isn't over yet. We'll be pushing on in the morning."

"How far?" Cantey asked.

"All the way to the Elbe," Purdue said.

And indeed, by nightfall, the 120th Regiment

with their attached 823rd TD Battalion had made substantial progress. Not only had they annihilated the 60th Grenadier Regiment, but the FJR 6 Parachute Regiment as well. Only Lt. Col. Friherr von der Heydte, Gen. Walter Gericke, commander of the 2nd Parachute Division, Maj. Sepp Krafft, and a few other officers had escaped with their enlisted men after the Americans had overrun Kirchhellen. By midnight, 25 March, both this town and Hunxe had fallen, and German survivors had retreated northeastward into the Ruhr Valley.

In the northern sector, Col. Jim Coutts had taken the GIs of his 513th Parachute Regiment along the Wesel-Dorsten railroad pike, while troops of the 6th Canadian Brigade moved in a parallel column along the Wesel-Dorsten highway. The mixed Canadian-American troops pushed on toward Gahlen, where the surviving regiments of General Caseman's 84th German Infantry Division had been joined by a battalion of troops from the 15th Panzer Division that had rushed southward from Borken. Caseman had posted sentinels on the north and east approaches to Gahlen, hoping to stop any Allied attempt to take the village.

About two miles from Gahlen, Colonel Coutts met with the Canadian 6th Brigade commander. They decided that the Americans would attack the town from the east, while the Canadians attacked from the north. By early afternoon of 25 March, the Allied troops had come within a mile of their objective to make the simultaneous assaults. Lt. Dave McGuire, now acting commander of E Company after the death of Captain Kenyon, marched his company through a wooded area to launch the initial 513th Regiment attack.

Inside the trees, John Queenan led his men cautiously through the gloomy forest. The GIs were tense. They expected at any moment to get raked with sniper fire or hit with shellfire from hidden German artillery pieces. But, Queenan's platoon met no resistance inside the trees, and they emerged on the eastern side of the brake without having fired a shot. However, once the GIs emerged from the trees and exposed themselves, the Germans opened with 88mm guns in a rolling barrage. The screaming shells erupted in a neat row at the edge of the trees and the GIs scattered.

"Cover! Take cover!" Queenan screamed.

GIs then scampered into recently gouged 88mm shellholes.

"Son of a bitch," Private Hines cursed. "They're never gonna stop. Why the hell don't they just give up? They ain't got a prayer, anyway."

"Stay down," Pfc. Walt Leonard cried before he cowered in the hole to avoid shrapnel from another nearby shell explosion.

"This is crazy, crazy," Paul Hines raved on. "The bastards have to quit or get killed. Why the hell are they givin' us all this grief?"

Then, as so often happened when the Germans opened with artillery, the Americans responded in kind, and with more devastating effects. Col. Jim Coutts called for air support, while he moved his 105mm guns into position to return fire. Heavy U.S. shells soon took a toll, blowing away some of the German defenses, flattening buildings inside Gahlen, setting armored vehicles afire, and pounding 88mm guns into twisted metal.

Then Coutts moved his troops forward, with Sergeant Queenan's 1st Platoon in the van. However, Queenan and his men suddenly stopped and hugged the ground when machine gun fire chattered from one of the battered buildings inside the village. During a momentary lull, Queenan peeked in front of him. He then called artillery liaison. "The building right next to the road. There's a machine gun nest holding us up. Knock it out."

"Will do," the artillery officer answered.

A moment later, a 75mm TD shell hit the building squarely disintegrating the machine gun nest and half a wall. Queenan then gestured to his men and the GIs zigzagged quickly forward until they reached the town itself. When more machine gun fire came from an equally smashed building across from an intersection littered with debris, the GIs ducked behind a wall.

"Jesus Christ," Ralph Walley complained, "they're holed up all over this town."

"Looks like it," the platoon non-com said. Once more he picked up his radio and asked for artillery support. However, when a TD rumbled up the street, the sergeant gestured to the driver.

"Right in that building; another machine gun position."

Seconds later, a 75mm shell from the TD hit squarely on target. Three Germans dropped from the battered floor of the building like falling rocks. Queenan then led his GIs forward again. "Move it! Let's move it!"

The GIs crouched behind the TD that rumbled slowly up the street, while the armored vehicle's gunners swung their 75mm barrel from left to right. Soon enough, another chatter of machine gun fire erupted, the slugs ricochetting off the hard surface of the TD in a rattle of pings. The gunner sent a 75mm shell whizzing in the direction of the enemy fire and once more an explosion silenced a German position.

As the TD moved into another street, a sudden 88mm shell exploded in front of the vehicle, ripping apart the front end and setting the TD afire. The GIs behind the vehicle scattered, while the burning crew attempted to scramble out of the flames. They died from searing fire before they escaped. Their burning flesh sent a noxious, foul smelling odor into the ranks of the 1st Platoon, and the GIs felt nauseous. Then, another 88mm shell erupted next to the flaming TD and knocked down the wall of a gutted structure. A cascade of debris fell onto the troops, leaving four men dead and six wounded amid the rubble.

"Medic!" Sergeant Queenan cried.

Before medics arrived, Private Hines, Private Walley, and Private Leonard hurried to the half buried GIs. The trio cast aside the dead and dragged out the wounded before treating them with sulfa powder and then binding their wounds.

Another 88mm shell exploded and turned more segments of gutted buildings into powdered rubble. Fortunately, the burst had not killed or maimed any more men from 1st Platoon. Sergeant Queenan frantically called for artillery support. "You've got to stop that eighty-eight or we'll all be killed."

"Where is it?" the artillery liaison non-com asked.

"I don't know. Somewhere up the street."

"We've got to know where it is, Sergeant."

"Goddamn it, just send a barrage up the street; you'll hit it. Get that barrage up there."

"Okay, okay."

A moment later, a pair of 90mm mobile guns sent a walking barrage up the street in front of 1st Platoon. The explosions knocked down more walls from the shells of wrecked buildings, tore up more holes in the rubbled streets, and killed more Germans hidden among the craggy recesses of this once quaint German village. One shell apparently hit the 88mm gun because when the American artillery fire ceased, no more enemy shells came toward the Americans.

Queenan and his dogfaces continued on, ducking into buildings to search cellars, battered rooms, dark lofts, and other areas where Germans might be hiding to avoid the Americans, or to pick off GIs. For more than an hour the dogfaces continued their tedious chore, often becoming victims of grenade explosions, burp gun fire, or simple rifle shots. But finally, Queenan and his platoon cleared an entire street of Germans and the sergeant sat down to rest. The day had now darkened into dusk and Queenan took count. He had lost eight men killed and twelve wounded, including Private Hines who had suffered a hit in the shoulder.

For their efforts in two days of fighting, Boures and Walley won Silver Stars; Hines and Leonard won Bronze Stars. During the last fighting, Pvt. Ralph Walley, the Little Rock, Arkansas, native, had kicked open a door to a room in a battered building and got hit with two slugs from a burp gun. Before he fell and died, Walley had killed the Germans and saved his platoon from death or injury from these snipers. Walley's Silver Star was awarded posthumously.

Other platoons from other companies among the 513th Parachute Regiment had also worked their way through the village of Gahlen. These GIs had also darted in and out of wrecked buildings to hunt down Germans, killing or capturing them. Meanwhile, more TDs from the tank battalion also rumbled over debris-clogged streets, occasionally exchanging shell fire with German artillerymen or knocking out machine gun or sniper posts.

And during the course of the afternoon, P-47 fighter-bombers roared over Gahlen on three occasions, unleashing their 5" rockets and 250 pound bombs. The American airmen killed and maimed more Germans, destroyed more equipment, and knocked out several 88mm and 76mm guns.

By dark, Col. Jim Coutts stood on the outskirts of Gahlen and stared at the autobahn about two miles off. The 513th and the Canadians had taken this important objective. "What are the casualties?" Coutts asked.

Capt. Oscar Fodder, still hobbling on his wounded leg, came next to Coutts. "We lost about fifty men killed and a hundred wounded since we left this morning."

"Goddamn it," Coutts cursed.

"The Germans are tough, sir," Lt. Col. Allen Miller said. "Some of them fought like demons."

"How many prisoners?"

"We took about six hundred and so far we've counted about five hundred enemy dead."

"That's only a thousand men," Coutts huffed. "They were supposed to have a couple of regiments here."

"The rest of them got away," Miller said. "They're retreating northeast and I don't think we should chase them in the dark. God knows what they might have in the trees, and our flyboys can't do us much good at night."

Big Jim Coutts nodded. Then he sighed. "Okay, we'll bivouac here for the night, but make sure you've got plenty of posted sentinels. I don't want any krauts in here to slit a few throats. We'll start for Dorsten in the morning." The colonel squeezed his face. "That town will probably be full of goddamn Germans, too, so we may have a tough fight there, like we did here today."

"Yes sir," Miller said.

"Make sure all TD and mobile guns are cleaned and ready for new fire fights," Coutts continued. "Order the men to clean rifles and machine gun barrels. And try to ease them, so they'll get a good night's sleep. They'll need it."

"Yes sir," Miller said again.

A quiet soon descended with the darkness over Gahlen. In the night, the shell pocked buildings resembled grotesque black figurines. But most of the 513th Parachute GIs cuddled wherever they could amid the rubble: in lofts, in rooms without walls, or even in dark cellars. Such shelters beat the hard damp earth under pup tents. After the evening meal, tired and spent, the GIs curled under blankets and most of them fell asleep quickly. Between the physical and mental anguish of this second day, slumber came easily.

Only sentinels stood awake through the night. But they had no need to worry. Every last German who could move had hurried off to the eastward.

CHAPTER FOURTEEN

The battle for Wesel was perhaps the most bitter of Operation Plunder. In other areas, when the worst came, the German troops could flee eastward. However in the Rhine riverbank city, Colonel Ross, his Volkstrum soldiers, and the experienced paratroop cadres had nowhere to run so they fought viciously.

Like other regimental commanders, Col. Jim Pierce also awoke early on this second day. Most of the stragglers from yesterday's landings had now joined the 194th, while armored vehicle and gun units of the 681st Glider Artillery had also joined. Lieutenant Colonel Keating, the 681st commander, had sent off one battalion to join the 513th Regiment, and the others would join the 194th on the march to Wesel. Further the big

U.S. Liberators accommodated Pierce with more supplies, when the B-24s came over the American positions at 0630 hours to drop rations, ammo, medicine, and other provisions.

The B-24s came in low, just over the treetops. So many of the supply parachutes had barely opened before the cartons hit the ground. During the morning drop, the 2nd Air Division's B-24s ran into heavy flak and the Americans lost three Liberators. One heavy bomber caught a flak hit that chopped off the left wing, and the aircraft simply flipped over. Another victim of AA fire burst into flames and crashed in a fiery ball, while a third B-24 caught a point blank 88mm burst in the tail and the plane plopped into the trees.

But still the squadron of Liberators had dropped enough provisions for at least two days, so Colonel Pierce could move in on Wesel with plenty of muscle.

Inside Wesel, Col. Frederick Ross had established defenses throughout the city. He had already been fighting furiously against Canadian troops that had struck the northwest defenses, and against 119th Regiment troops of the U.S. 30th Infantry Division that had attacked the southern perimeter of the city. Now Ross faced a third assault from the northeast.

Within a mile of Wesel, two battalions of artillery and armor from the 681st joined the 194th Glider troops. Jim Pierce held up his column again to formulate infantry-armor teams. In addition, Pierce ordered L-5 Piper cubs to reconnoiter the enemy defense from the air, while he himself peered through his field glasses at the German defenses. Then at 0900 hours, he met with his commanders.

"They're well dug in here," he pointed to a spot on a chart, "and we'll need artillery barrages to clean them out or chase them off before we move in."

"Okay," Lieutenant Colonel Keating said.

"I want a rolling barrage," Pierce said, "and we'll repeat the process a few times before we attack."

At 0915 hours, more than twenty U.S. 90mm and 105mm mobile guns opened on the German defenses. Numbing explosions erupted about the northeast areas of the city, knocking down more of the shattered buildings, chopping up German gun emplacements, and shattering many of the Volkstrum Division trenches. Only sporadic 76mm gunfire responded to the heavy American barrage that soon covered with a mass of fire and smoke the entire German defense sector.

"Okay, let's move in," Pierce said.

The glider troops now crouched forward, ducking behind TDs and Sherman tanks that rumbled ahead. Sgt. Bill Woolfort led a squad of men on the left in S/Sgt. Tom Martin's 1st Platoon. The men were tense, because they knew that heavy shelling and bombing attacks had often failed to destroy enemy defenses, and German troops were often waiting to hit advancing dogfaces quite hard.

"Stay alert," Martin said. "We gave them a

good pasting with artillery, but they might still be there."

"We'll be careful," Sergeant Woolfort said.

But as the Sherman tanks entered the city and growled over a rubbled avenue, the GIs met no resistance. Sergeant Martin saw no sign of the enemy in the eerie quiet of the battered streets that stretched for block after block. Only the heavy hum of M-4 tank engines and the steady clang of their treads broke the uneasy silence. Martin did not like it. He suspected that the Germans were somewhere up ahead and waiting to hit the advancing column viciously when the GIs came into close range.

The platoon sergeant had guessed right.

Martin's soldiers had trudged behind four Sherman tanks for about 20 minutes when an 88mm artillery gun boomed from somewhere to the east inside the devastated city. The German shells exploded with numbing accuracy, quickly knocking out two of the Sherman tanks, while hot shrapnel killed six men in the platoon and injured eight more.

"Cover!" Martin cried.

Woolfort also cried. "Take cover!"

The GIs ran for shelter behind the walls of gutted buildings and slumped to the ground, their hearts pounding. They cowered again when more 88mm shells exploded off to their left, fortunately too far away to cause further casualties.

"We got to knock out those goddamn guns," Woolfort said.

"Sure," Martin huffed, "and how do you suggest we do that? We don't even know where the hell they are."

Before Woolfort answered, two more German shells whooshed overhead and the subsequent explosions luckily erupted behind the GIs and none of the dogfaces caught shrapnel. However, Martin knew he could not stay here and wait, for sooner or later, enemy shells would catch them. He called battalion headquarters.

"There's an eighty-eight ahead of us causing all kinds of damage," the platoon non-com said. "They've mauled our unit and knocked out a couple of Shermans. If you don't get that gun, they'll annihilate us."

"Do you know its location?"

"All I know — it's up the street."

"Okay, I'll get a Piper on it."

A moment later, an L-5 plane circled over the town and the pilot caught the flash from the 88mm just as the weapon unleashed another shell toward Sergeant Martin's platoon. The pilot quickly radioed the 681st Artillery liaison officer. A moment later, a barrage of 105mm shells screamed into Wesel and exploded in a staccato of deafening blasts several blocks up the street from Martin. More walls collapsed, dust and debris rose high in the air, fires erupted, and smoke rose for several hundred feet.

Sergeant Martin warily left his shelter and peered through his field glasses into the holocaust up ahead. But he saw nothing except the heavy mist of dust and smoke.

"I think they got the bastards," Martin told

Woolfort.

"I hope so," the squad sergeant said.

"Okay, let's move out."

"Jesus, Tom, we only got two Shermans left."

"I'll call for more armor."

Martin led his platoon cautiously up the street, sidestepping mounds of debris, or plodding over heaps of fallen bricks and powdered mortar from smashed buildings. Soon the GIs reached the glob of smashed buildings where only wisps of smoke now rose upward. The GIs probed through the rubble: three twisted 88mm guns and 14 dead German artillerymen, some of whose faces still wore looks of terrified surprise. Martin and his dogfaces did not find a single one of the German soldiers still alive.

"Christ, those 105s did a job on them," Woolfort said.

"We'll keep going, but we'll stay alert," Martin answered.

The GIs moved on for another two blocks, when sudden rifle pops greeted the Americans. Once more the 1st Platoon scattered, escaping the sniper fire before anybody got hit. Martin again studied the area with field glasses and caught movement on the second floor of one of the buildings and on the third floor of a second ravaged building.

"I think I know where those krauts are," the platoon sergeant said. He turned to one of his GIs. "Aim your bazooka right at that second floor window, the third one from the left."

A moment later the bazooka shell exploded,

ripping out a chunk of the building, including the paneless window. Two German soldiers tumbled down with the debris and plopped into the rubbled street below. A moment later, the bazooka man aimed his barrel at a third story window at a second building, and he once more squeezed the trigger. Again a subsequent explosion blew away a segment of the building and dropped two more German soldiers into the street below.

"Okay," Martin gestured, "keep moving."

"Jesus Christ," the bazooka man complained, "how far do we have to go?"

"Until we meet up with the Canadians."

"Christ, when will that be?"

"I don't know," Martin shrugged. "Maybe an hour; maybe not for another day."

"Goddamn it," another GI cursed. "Another day?"

But despite the grumbling, the platoon plodded on, crouching behind two Shermans and another pair of light tanks that had come up to replace the two disabled M-4s. The soldiers trudged ahead for another half hour without incident, but soon, they again met resistance. A rattle of machine gun fire from two directions echoed from a pair of buildings. Fortunately, the slugs merely pinged off the thick steel walls of the U.S. tanks and failed to hit any of the GIs behind the American armored vehicles.

"Get the bastards! Get those krauts!" Martin cried.

When another chatter of machine gun fire echoed across ruined Wesel, two tank gunners whirled their 75mm barrels into position and then fired. The close range blasts tore down whatever remained of the two buildings that had sheltered the machine gunners. The Germans and their guns had been so thoroughly buried in the collapsing brick and mortar that the Americans did not even see a sign of the slain German snipers.

Martin's platoon moved on, once more stepping gingerly over rubble, and once more keeping a sharp watch for snipers or hidden machine gun teams. And again, only two blocks later, a new chatter of machine gun fire rattled from a pair of windows. This time, the Germans showed more finesse. They waited for the growling tanks to pass them before opening on the trailing GIs. The chatter of fire dropped five men before others scurried to the left side of the tanks for shelter.

Six wounded GIs in the same burst of machine gun fire now flopped about the street in agony as the enemy gun still sprayed the street. Sgt. Bill Woolfort licked his lips and then turned to Martin. "I got to get those guys out of there. Cover me."

Martin did not answer. He only nodded soberly.

The GIs opened fire with BAR and rifles in the direction of the machine gun fire, while Woolfort slithered over the street like a giant caterpillar. Occasional fire from the Germans chopped up pops of pavement, but Woolfort quickly dragged one of the wounded back to safety behind a tank.

Then, again and again, while GIs exchanged fire with the Germans, the squad sergeant continued to crawl into the open to carry back his wounded comrades. He was just hauling the last of the six wounded when a machine gun bullet caught him in the shoulder. He winced in pain as blood saturated his soiled fatigue uniform and he stopped his slithering movement. However, S/Sgt. Tom Martin moved out from his shelter with a pair of soldiers and the trio dragged Woolfort and this last wounded man to shelter. Sgt. Bill Woolfort, for his gallant effort, would win a Distinguished Service Cross.

"Medic! Medic!" Martin cried.

"We're here, Sarge."

"Get these wounded to the rear."

"I've already called for jeep litter carriers," the medic said. "They'll be moving up to carry them to an aid station. They should be here soon."

Meanwhile, two of the Sherman tanks had spun 90 degrees and now aimed their 75mm barrels toward the buildings across the street. But the firing had stopped.

"What the hell do we do now, Sarge?" one of the platoon soldiers asked. "They don't even know where those krauts are."

"We'll just knock down the whole goddamn block," Martin said. He ordered the tank crew to do just that. The Sherman gunners then unleashed a barrage of 75mm shells at point blank range, bringing down the walls of the buildings like cascading waterfalls. If there had been German machine gunners hidden in these buildings,

247

they had disappeared in the debris of collapsing structures brought on by the fusillade of tank shells.

Martin's platoon continued on, still running into occasional resistance. BAR men, bazooka men, and the tank gunners usually took care of snipers or enemy machine gunners, while the L-5 Piper Cubs pointed from the air the enemy's big guns that were subsequently knocked out by 681st 90mm or 105mm or zooming fighter-bombers. Martin's platoon also ducked in and out of the battered buildings, probing through rooms, cellars, corridors, attics, or rooftops where Germans might have been hiding. During their sweep, the platoon killed about 50 Germans and captured about 50 more.

Not only Martin and his platoon fought their way through the streets of northeast Wesel. Other 194th Glider troops had been making the same kinds of sweeps, also knocking out German machine gun nests, destroying field pieces, and eliminating Volkstrum snipers. Almost continually, big U.S. artillery from mobile guns of the Sherman tanks laced suspected or verified German defenses to snuff out resistance. L-5s hung over the Wesel battleground to pinpoint strong points for American artillery or U.S. P-47 fighter-bombers that pummelled the Volkstrum Division troops with both demolition and incendiary bombs.

For nearly four hours the dogfaces of the 194th fought their way through the streets, while Canadians fought their way through the city from the west, and the 119th Regiment of the 30th U.S. Division struggled through battered Wesel from the south. By midafternoon, the Allied forces had forced the Volkstrum troops into a small four block pocket. Col. Frederick Ross had tried desperately to hold off further Canadian and American advances, but the truth was now evident — his plight was hopeless.

S/Sgt. Tom Martin's own platoon had reached the German commander's last outpost, a CP in the basement of a shell pocked library. Several German machine gun teams had opened fire on the advancing Shermans, but the M-4s responded with 75mm shell fire that had blown away almost half of the building. The Germans inside were hopelessly trapped.

In fact, when shrapnel from one of the American shells left a deep laceration in Colonel Ross's leg, his staff pleaded with him to surrender. They insisted the defenders would only lose more men in a senseless fight. Ross hesitated, but as Sherman tanks prepared to fire more 75mm shells into the library, he acquiesced and sent two officers from the building with white flags.

S/Sgt. Tom Martin stood upright and shouted. "Kommen aus!"

The German officers nodded and then led 229 Germans out of the building, including the limping Colonel Ross, commander of the Wesel Volkstrum Division.

Wesel was finished and so was Ross's division. By late afternoon of 25 March, all fighting in the battered city on the bank of the Rhine had come to an end. Thus the loss of Wesel had joined the loss of Dinslaken, Hunxe, Gahlen in the east, Kirchhellen in the southeast, and Hamminkeln and Isselburg in the north. The combined British-American-Canadian forces had cleansed the entire objective east of the Rhine, a patch of heavily defended terrain that measured some 25 miles in depth and 30 miles in length.

Now Field Marshal Sir Bernard Montgomery looked to the east, at Dorsten, Borken, and the Ruhr Valley beyond. He urged his division commanders to make their thrusts as quickly as possible.

The Germans, however, were not yet ready to quit, despite the serious losses in the oblong pocket east of the Rhine. Field Marshal Blaskowitz mustered whatever remained of his troops, armor, and guns to defend Dorsten in the southern sector and Borken in the northeast sector. The remnants of the 116th Panzer and 2nd Parachute Divisions had dug in around Borken. Further, Maj. Walter Kowakoski and the AR 234 jet bombers of his KG 51 attacked American positions during the day 26 March, while Lt. Col. Johannes Steinhoff led his ME 262 jet fighter-bombers against British positions on 26 March.

The jet air attacks did not cause any real physical damage, but the blows did cause psychological uneasiness in the GIs and Tommies.

But then on the morning of 27 March, after the

U.S. 9th Air Force recon planes found the jet airfields in northwest Germany, squadrons of B-24 heavy bombers and B-26 medium bombers roared over the areas and dropped 1,250 tons of bombs on the airfields. If the U.S. air assaults did not destroy all of the jet aircraft, the Americans had so badly gouged the runways that jet aircraft could not take off. Further, the 9th Air Force conducted almost daily bombing runs to keep the runways disabled and the jet planes grounded.

Meanwhile, other 9th Air Force bombers and fighter-bombers intensified their air support for American ground troops, while the British 2nd Tactical Air Force continually supported British troops to the north.

The town of Dorsten became a heavy battleground on the morning of 27 March, with the Germans fighting viciously, despite continued poundings by American ground troops, armor, field guns, and aircraft. In fact, the Germans held there for two days before their defenses finally collapsed and the battered Germans retreated eastward. On 28 March, American troops overran Dorsten, where the men of the 30th Infantry Division again saw the autobahn in the distance.

"We'll start moving over that highway tomorrow," Gen. Leland Hobbs, the division commander, told Colonel Purdue of the 120th Regiment. "You and your boys did a goddamn good job, Branner, and you and your men deserve some rest, but we can't stop now."

"No sir," Purdue said.

To the north, Gen. Bud Wiley of the 17th Airborne had thrown his 513th and 507th Regiments against Borken, supported by a brigade of troops from the British 51st Highlanders. For two days, the combined American-British force assailed the strategic highway road junction, 25 miles northeast of Wesel. Borken was the last German outpost guarding the flat, open Ruhr plains, so the Germans fought tenaciously. However, on 29 March, the German defenses finally crumbled and GIs of the 17th Airborne and Tommies of the 51st Highlanders marched through the battered, abandoned town.

GIs of the 194th Glider Infantry, meanwhile, had raced eastward beyond Gahlen to the town of Lembeck where German defenders had entrenched themselves in the Lembeck Castle to halt the Americans. Colonel Pierce pummelled the defenders with heavy tank and mobile artillery fire, while P-47s once more plastered an enemy target from the air. By midafternoon, the GIs prepared to overrun the castle and its defenders.

Sgt. Clint Hedrick of the 194th's C Company led his 3rd Platoon within 200 yards of the castle, whose moat had long ago dried up and become filled with dirt and brush. The GIs opened on the Germans with machine guns and BAR fire, but the Germans responded with machine gun fire of their own.

"We're stuck here, Sarge," a GI told Hedrick.

"Just cover me," Hedrick said.

The GI nodded and Hedrick brazenly moved forward, almost into the very jaws of the machine gun nest. "Kommen aus!" the sergeant cried. "Aufgeben!"

The Germans were shocked to see the brazen American sergeant so close to their machine gun nest to demand their surrender. For a moment, they stood aghast, but then, one of them sent a rat-a-tat of machine fire at Sgt. Clint Hedrick. The U.S. platoon leader caught several hits that ripped open his chest before blood exploded from his breast. However as Hedrick fell, he sent a chatter of BAR fire into the nest and killed all three of the Wehrmacht soldiers. Then, while the sergeant collapsed to the ground, the men of his platoon raced forward and overran the nest, thus making the first breach in the Lembeck defenses. Within an hour, the 194th Glider troops captured the castle to open still another path to the autobahn.

Sgt. Clint M. Hedrick died from his wounds after his heroic action, but he had wedged a path for other GIs. He won a posthumous Congressional Medal of Honor, the third GI from the 17th Airborne Division to be so honored during Operation Plunder.

On 31 March, with the Rhine pocket secured, Field Marshal Montgomery held up his advance to regroup before he continued his thrust into the Ruhr Valley, the industrial heart of northwest Germany.

Field Marshal Blaskowitz, whose Wesel defenses east of the Rhine had collapsed, now led the tattered remnants of his Army Group H in a northeasterly retreat through the Ruhr Valley. Blaskowitz had lost nearly 5,000 men killed and 6,400 captured during the five day battle. He had lost more than 100 tanks and some 200 field pieces, from 76mm to 88mm. He suffered an additional 20,000 men wounded, and he had lost every strategic strong point to hold off an Allied thrust into the open Ruhr Valley.

For the Americans, the toll had also been quite heavy. The 17th Airborne Division had suffered 223 men killed, 695 wounded, and 666 missing during the five day struggle, while the 30th and 79th Infantry Divisions had lost 278 men killed, 786 wounded, and 375 missing. The Americans had also lost 40 Sherman tanks and more than 50 field pieces.

The American Air Force had not escaped unscathed, either. The U.S. 2nd Air Division had lost 23 B-24s from AA fire while the Liberator squadrons were dropping supplies to U.S. paratroopers and glider troops. However, the B-24s had dropped over 20,000 tons of provisions to keep the U.S. combat troops in business. The 9th Air Force had lost four medium bombers and 17 fighter-bombers during the five day campaign.

All three American divisions, the 79th, 30th, and 17th, won Distinguished Unit Citations for their efforts in Operation Plunder that had opened the way into the Ruhr Valley.

In fact, by 1 April, the Allied 21st Army Group was speeding through northwest Germany, and by 13 April they had trapped the German Army Group H at Oldenbert on the west bank of the Elbe River. Here, the Germans faced annihilation or a retreat into Russian hands on the east bank of the River. Blaskowitz wisely chose to surrender his forces to the British and Americans. The Allies captured an astounding 316,930 German soldiers, including soldiers of the 25th Army, the 1st Parachute Army, the 7th Panzer Army and Luftflotte II.

Among the prisoners surrendering to the British and Americans were Field Marshal Blaskowitz himself, Gen. Walter Gericke of the 2nd Parachute Division, Gen. Zengen Waldenberg of the 116th Panzer Division, Gen. Edward Caseman of the 84th Infantry Division, Col. Friherr von der Heydte of the FJR 6 Regiment, Maj. Sepp Krafft of the 60th Grenadiers, Lt. Col. Johannes Steinhoff of the JV 7 jet unit, and Maj. Walter Kowakoski of the KG 51 jet unit.

Only two weeks after Blaskowitz surrendered, the entire German military disintegrated. On 6 May 1945, the war in Europe came to an end.

PARTICIPANTS
Operation Plunder

Allied:

ETO—Commander in chief—Gen. Dwight Eisenhower

21st Army Group—Field Marshal Bernard Montgomery

1st Allied Airborne Army—Gen. Lewis Brereton

American:

30th Infantry Division—Gen. Leland Hobbs

    120th Regiment—Col. Branner Purdue

        2nd Battalion—Lt. Col. Ed Cantey

    119th Regiment—Lt. Col. Norman King

    117th Regiment—Col. Walter Warner

17th Airborne Division—Gen. Bud Miley

    513th Regiment—Col. James Coutts

2nd Battalion—Lt. Col. Allen Miller
1st Battalion—Maj. Paul Smith
507th Regiment—Col. Edwin Roff
194th Glider Regiment—Col. James Pierce
C Company—Capt. Fred Wittig
E Company—Capt. H.A. Lyerly
F Company—Capt. Robert Dukes
681st Glider Infantry Artillery—Col. Joseph Keating
79th Infantry Division—Gen. Ira Wyck
British:
6th Airborne Division, 51st Highlander Division, 3rd Infantry Division, 33rd Welsh Division, and 15th Scottish Division.
Also: 1st Canadian Brigade and 6th Canadian Brigade.
9th Air Force—Gen. Hoyt Vandenberg
354th Fighter Group—Col. George Bickel

German:
Army Group H—Field Marshal Johannes Blaskowitz
1st Parachute Army—Gen. Alfred Schlemm
2nd Parachute Division—Gen. Walter Gericke
FJR 6 Regiment—Col. Friherr von der Heydte
7th Parachute Division—Gen. Eugene Meindle
8th Parachute Division—Gen. Ludwig Heilman
25th Army—Gen. Gunther Blementritt
Wesel Volkstrum Division—Col. Frederick Ross

84th Division—Gen. Edward Caseman
116th Panzer Division—Gen. Zengen Walden-
　　berg
70th Grenadier Regiment—Col. Walter Har-
　　zer
Also: 15th Panzer Division and 180th Infantry
　　Division
Luftflotte II—Gen. Erick Wilke
JV 7—Lt. Col. Johannes Steinhoff
KG 51—Maj. Walter Kowakoski

BIBLIOGRAPHY

BOOKS:

Blond, George, *Death of Hitler's Germany,* Mac-Millan & Co., New York City, 1954.

Bradley, Omar, *A Soldier's Story,* Henry Holt & Co., New York City, 1951.

Brereton, Lewis, *The Brereton Diary,* Wm. Morrow & Co., New York City, 1946.

Churchill, Winston, *Triumph and Tragedy, Vol. VI,* Houghton-Mifflin Co., New York City, 1953.

Edwards, Roger, *German Airborne Troops,* Doubleday & Co., Garden City, N.Y., 1974.

Eisenhower, Dwight, *Crusade in Europe,* Doubleday & Co., New York City, 1948.

Eisenhower, John S.D., *The Bitter Woods,* P.G. Putnam & Son, New York City, 1969.

McDonald, Charles B., *The Last Offensive,* Office of the Chief of Military History, U.S. Army, Washington, DC, 1973.

Montgomery, Sir Bernard, *Normandy to the Baltic,* Houghton-Mifflin Co., New York City, 1948.

Simpson, W.H., *Conquer, the Story of the 9th Army,* Infantry Journal Press, Washington, DC, 1947.

Stacey, C.P., *The Victory Campaign,* Queens Printers Pub., Ottawa, Can., 1966.

Wilmot, Chester, *The Struggle for Europe,* Harper & Row, New York City, 1952.

ARCHIVE SOURCES

Military Archives, GSA, Washington National Records Center, Washington, DC.

SHAEF Files: #311-III-Plunder

Historical Study #97, Dr. John Warren, 9th Air Force Operations (Plunder)

1st Allied Airborne Army, Operation Plunder, dated 19 May 1944, narrative, "Mission Accomplished"

Manuscript Narratives:
Rhine Crossing by the 30th Infantry Division
30th Division Special Report
30th Division G-3 JNL File, 26-28 March 1945
17th Airborne Division History, 15 April 1943-16 September 1945

Regimental Action Reports:
120th Infantry Regiment, March 1945
513th Parachute Regiment

FO Order #16, Plunder, 17 March 1945
Action reports for March 24, March 25,
March 26, March 27, March 28, and
March 29, 1945
194th Glider Regiment narrative report, 24
March-30 March 1945, "Invasion of Germany"

German Monograph Records (ATIS) Allied
Translator & Interpreter Section
MSS #B-414 Army Group H (B Nordwest) 15
March-9 May 1945
MSS #B-593 The Battles of Army Group H
(Gen. Karl Wagener)
MSS #B-416 XLVII Corps — 8 March-16 April
1945
MSS #B-674 — Gen. der Infantrie Guenther
Blementritt
MSS #B-198 — Gen. Walter Gericke

Photos: All photos from Still Picture Branch,
National Archives, Washington , DC; Defense
Audio Visual Agency, Pentagon, Washington,
DC; Govt. Bildarchives, W. Germany,
Koblenz, Germany

Maps: from Army Map Service, National Archives, Washington, DC

Note: The author would like to thank Mr. Fred Purnell and Mrs. Victoria Washington of the Washington National Records Center for their help in obtaining for me the many volumes of research material that proved invaluable in completing this book.

McLEANE'S RANGERS
by John Darby

THE SURVIVALIST SERIES
by Jerry Ahern

ZEBRA WINS THE WEST
WITH THESE EXCITING BESTSELLERS!

PISTOLERO   (1331, $2.25)
by Walt Denver
Death stalks the dusty streets of Belleville when a vicious power
struggle tears the town in half. But it isn't until a beautiful rancher's
daughter gets trapped in a bloody crossfire that someone with cold
nerve and hot lead goes into action. Only who would've guessed
that a stranger would be the one to put his life on the line to save
her?

RED TOMAHAWK   (1362, $2.25)
by Jory Sherman
Soon, deep in the Dakotas—at a place called Little Big Horn—Red
Tomahawk will discover the meaning of his tribe's fateful vision.
And the Sioux will find a greatness in his enduring legend that will
last through all time!

BLOOD TRAIL SOUTH   (1349, $2.25)
by Walt Denver
Five years have passed since six hardcases raped and murdered
John Rustin's wife, butchered his son, and burned down his ranch.
Now, someone with cold eyes and hot lead is after those six coyotes.
Some say he's a lawman. Others say—in a low whisper—that it's
John Rustin himself!

*Available wherever paperbacks are sold, or order direct from the
Publisher. Send cover price plus 50¢ per copy for mailing and
handling to Zebra Books, 475 Park Avenue South, New York, N.Y.
10016. DO NOT SEND CASH.*